A CANDLELIGHT ROMANCE

CANDLELIGHT ROMANCES

FORBIDDEN
BLESSING

Lucy Casselman

A CANDLELIGHT ROMANCE

Published by
Dell Publishing Co., Inc.
1 Dag Hammarskjold Plaza
New York, New York 10017

Dell ® TM 681510, Dell Publishing Co., Inc.

ISBN: 0-440-12638-X

Printed in the United States of America

First printing—August 1980

FORBIDDEN
BLESSING

CHAPTER ONE

Sara Ann Williston watched curiously as the pretty black girl behind the customs desk glanced up at her, then back to her passport, found it satisfactory, and resolutely stamped her approval.

"Welcome to the British Virgin Islands," said the girl as though she meant it.

As Sara passed to another counter and identified her bag, a beefy man pushed his way up to the front. In a loud, grating voice he said to Sara, "Big improvement here. Last time they had an open shed—rain all over everything. But they're still slow as molasses. Hey, buddy! I'm next."

The customs man, neat in sharply pressed khaki, said softly, "This lady is next, sir. Please open your bag, miss."

Sara fumbled with the lock on her bag. This was her first trip outside the United States, and she felt somewhat nervous. Connecticut seemed a world away from the Beef Island airport and the other sun-drenched islands of the British Virgin Islands. Where was Great Camanoe? she wondered.

The customs man held up two gaily wrapped packages. He looked politely to Sara for a clue.

"Christmas presents," she explained.

For two people whom she did not know and felt faintly apprehensive about meeting. The world, of course, knew Michelle Martine. Once a famous model, now older, she had turned to designing. Michelle had invited Sara to stay at the Martine house over Christmas and to stay on to help her in the new shop she was opening in Road Town on Tortola. She had also offered Sara a temporary job sketching her collection.

Michelle Martine lived with her brother, Mac. Both were friends of Sara's young stepmother, Gwen. Gwen had engineered both the job and the Christmas invitation, Sara suspected, in order to be alone with her new husband at Christmastime. Sara could easily understand Gwen's feelings, but she also felt like an outcast, cruelly excluded from the family on this important holiday. She would be alone on Christmas for the first time in all of her twenty-one years. Without family—and her father was all the family she had—it wouldn't seem like Christmas.

The customs man was still curiously examining the Christmas presents. He asked how much they were worth. Sara thought he was being rather cheeky, and she felt slightly embarrassed that they weren't worth a great amount.

"Worth?" Sara repeated, trying to remember. "One is a little nautical clock. About twelve dollars, I think. The other is a silk scarf. It was eighteen dollars."

The customs man nodded and replaced the gifts in her bag. "Diving gear," he said while continuing his search. "Fine water here," he told Sara with pride. "Paints?" He lifted his liquidy brown eyes to her violet-blue ones. "Bee-oo-ti-full scenery," he said with a wide toothy smile.

Having heard that customs men were curt, suspicious, and unsmiling, Sara smiled back with delight. Then a porter picked up her large Pullman case, and she followed him outside into eye-stinging sunshine, where a bevy of faded little taxis waited with their gesturing, chattering drivers.

The drivers spoke a sort of British English with an island lilt that made anything they said sound like a foreign language. Sara, already perspiring in her cotton pantsuit, brushed her wet forehead in confusion. The porter stood patiently beside her, still holding the heavy bag. Sara tipped him to ease his load, although he seemed not to mind staying with her. Drivers besieged her with offers and questions that she could hardly understand.

In the melee of departing tourists and the distracting noise, Sara saw no one that fit the description that her stepmother had given of the Martines: "When you see a couple of gorgeous blondes that look like twins. . . ." Sara glanced around anxiously.

A man as old as her father, but heavier, undoubtedly more affluent, and certainly more carefree, asked if he could be of any help.

Sara told him that she was being met by the Martines. Did he know them? He did not. She told him her destination.

"Great Camanoe," he repeated affably, as though she had mentioned a common friend. "Right across from Marina Cay, where we're going. Come along with us. We have to take a taxi to the jetty, and a boat will pick us up there. We can drop you at the Camanoe jetty."

Most of the tourists had departed by now, and still the Martines had not appeared. Sara accepted the man's kind offer and followed him to a taxi, where he introduced his daughter and her husband. When all of the bags had been stowed in a Jeep with a yellow-and-white-striped awning, they left for the jetty amid what could only be described as a holiday atmosphere. The young people, about Sara's age, held hands and jabbered excitedly. Sara wondered if they were on their honeymoon. But accompanied by the bride's father? Honeymoons were for two, a thought that reminded her once again, unhappily, of her father and his new bride.

At the jetty, while they waited for the launch, Sara saw awe-inspiring islands rising out of an impossibly blue sea: some green and mountainous, some sandy stretches no more than dunes with scrub, others like purple cones in the distance. Although Sara had studied a map of the British Virgin Islands before her trip, nothing seemed to be in the right place now. Perhaps she was too excited and mystified by her actual confrontation with such colorful natural beauty. All of it seemed so unspoiled, an Eden-like place, scarcely touched by civilization.

"Where is Great Camanoe?" she asked.

Her rescuer pointed to his left. "Over there. A fairly large island. You can't see it all from here. Marina Cay is right across the channel from your island."

"Are there many houses? It looks like a jungle."

"Only eleven on the whole island when I was here a few years back. Few more now, I expect." He waved enthusiastically at an approaching white launch. "There's our boat now."

Soon they were underway. The powerful surge of the boat as it plowed through the waves seemed to Sara like an animal being held in check. Strong winds hurled salt spray against her face, and Sara hoped the exhilarating boat ride would go on longer than it did. But her Good Samaritan pointed toward a large island on their portside.

"There's the Great Camanoe jetty." He said reassuringly, "You have arrived."

The launch's motors slowed, and the boat idled alongside the jetty long enough to transfer Sara and her luggage. She thanked them profusely and waved as they departed for Marina Cay across the channel.

A sudden feeling of loneliness took possession of Sara as she looked up toward the few rooftops that were visible on the rather mountainous island. Feeling as strange as a moon traveler, she lugged the heavy bag along the jetty, careful of her step because some boards were missing. Three boats were moored to the jetty, one rather large, the other two small and open.

No person was in sight. Near the jetty the only signs of civilization were a shelter of sorts with a wooden floor, and a small square cement-block building with an open door. She left her bag in the shelter and, hoping for a telephone, entered the square building. There was no phone, but a series of cubbyholes that looked like mailboxes with names beneath. She checked for Martine and found it: MacKinley and Michelle Martine. Progress, anyway. There was no mail in any of the boxes and no clue as to where the Martines might live.

Sara reflected bitterly that undoubtedly the Martines were not overly delighted about her visit, but this was a little more callous treatment than she had expected. Unless some mistake had been made in the information they received about her arrival time? Sara was always ready to give people the benefit of the doubt, and she very much wanted to believe the best about the Martines.

Three dirt roads appeared to extend from the jetty. On her left she could see that the road ended at a beach. To her right the road led along the water as far as she could see. Leading up the mountainside was the road that she decided to take, because although the rooftops were far apart, there seemed to be more of them in that direction. If the Martines did not live nearby, at least she could ask directions.

As Sara proceeded along the road she noticed that the island was not really as green as it looked from a distance. Cacti of various kinds reached out to stab her as she trudged along, and the roadside was bare and dry, but loaded with seashells. Stopping, she picked up a large brown and white mottled shell about three inches in diameter. It looked like an old snail shell and had a pearly interior. She put the shell in her pocket, a souvenir of this strange adventure. Sounds came from the underbrush near the road, and she thought of snakes, but saw nothing to justify her fears. Farther up the hill she turned to look for the water and was rewarded by a slash of incredible blue that sparkled through lacy green leaves.

Ahead, Sara saw what looked like a duststorm. A Jeep rocketed down the hill toward her, and she stepped quickly to the side of the road and waved, hoping to ask about the Martines. The Jeep, driven by a blond, deeply tanned, and mustachioed man in a battered planter's hat, screeched to a halt. A parrot, balanced precariously on his shoulder, teetered to gain its balance and squawked loudly in protest.

"Hello, stranger!" the man greeted her cheerfully.

"Hello! Can you tell me where the Martines live?"

"Well, I should think so! I'm Mac Martine."

"You *are*?" Sara exclaimed happily.

"In the flesh," he said, grinning and displaying a set of dazzling white, even teeth. "You wouldn't by any chance be—" He hesitated, giving her a roguish, incredulous look.

"I'm Sara Williston."

"Well, Sara! Get in and tell me how I happened to miss you at the airport. I was just on my way to meet you."

Sara needed no second invitation. The parrot on Mac Martine's shoulder scolded grumpily.

"Don't mind Captain Hook," Mac said. "He's getting old and crochety, but he means no harm. Where's your luggage?"

Sara had forgotten all about her bag. "In the shelter down by the jetty."

Mac put the Jeep in gear, and they bucketed down the hillside to the jetty. Mac swung her heavy bag into the backseat with ease.

"What you got in there anyway?" he asked curiously.

Sara laughed. "Really, I am not planning to stay forever. I didn't bring many clothes. But I heard about these waters and I had to bring my fins and mask. And I knew that I would want to paint, so I brought my supplies too."

Mac swiftly turned the Jeep around and headed back up the hill. "Good thinking," he said. "Michelle can be a bit of a slave driver. Had much experience in the designing racket?"

"None, but I can sketch. My father is an art professor, so I guess it comes naturally."

Mac turned and gave Sara a speculative glance. "Young *and* talented, eh?"

She replied modestly, "I don't know about that."

"So old Gwennie married your dad?"

"Old Gwennie? She's only six years older than I am."

"The age of consent," Mac said mockingly. "You seem younger."

Sara grimaced. "I'm not sure I should thank you for saying that."

"Nobody's ever happy," Mac complained. "The old want to be young, and the young are insulted because they don't look old." He lifted a hand from the wheel to tilt his ridiculous hat to an even more jaunty angle. "Now, how old do you think I am?"

Sara hated such questions. If she told him the truth and said that she thought he would be in his midthirties, he might be shocked. Especially if he was only twenty-eight. On the other hand, if she guessed too young, he would be equally shocked. She decided on "midthirties" as the best compromise.

He grinned. "Thirty-five, but I look younger, right? My sister, Michelle, is the same age, but she won't admit it. We're twins."

"Gwen told me to look for twins." Sara wondered why they lived together. Had neither of them ever wanted to leave the family home? Sara had been seriously thinking about getting a place of her own, especially now that Daddy and Gwen were married.

Mac seemed to sense her questions. "Michelle was married once," he said, "but she didn't like it."

"And you?" Sara asked politely.

"Never met a girl willing to save me from my lonely state of bachelorhood," he said with mock sorrow.

Sara doubted that, for he was quite handsome in a California-surfer way, and he had a practiced, light patter that amused and certainly must have attracted many girls. Also, according to Gwen, Mac Martine was a very wealthy young man, quite a catch for some lucky girl.

"*Voilà!* We have arrived," Mac announced as they pulled into a large courtyard.

The house had been carved out of the mountainside, it seemed, the back and kitchen patios an extension of the courtyard, where they parked. Mac deftly transferred Captain Hook to a large iron ring set on a post, evidently the parrot's home perch, for there was also food and water there. Hibiscus and other brilliant flowers framed the courtyard, and there were huge modern white pots of pink and red geraniums. A great banyan tree with a trunk about six feet in diameter stood in the center of the courtyard and shaded the whole area. Sara stood looking up into the enormous tree.

"They are beautiful, aren't they? Like big umbrellas."

Mac nodded. "Not too many of them around here.

Ever been to India?" Sara shook her head. "Sometimes one tree will shelter a whole village." He touched her arm lightly. "Come along—let's get you settled. You must be exhausted. Getting here is not easy, but once you arrive—"

"It's heaven!" Sara finished.

A thin, barefoot black man in khaki shorts and a starched white jacket came out to pick up Sara's bag.

"Thanks, John Paul," said Mac. "This is Miss Sara Williston. She will be in the Jasmine Room." He turned to Sara to explain. "We have named the bedrooms for flowers. There are six of them, and it's easier. Now let's find Michelle."

They entered the house through a double louvered door. Inside, the areas seemed to flow effortlessly into one another until they reached the loggia, and then the veranda that extended along the entire front of the house. Bedrooms flared from both sides of the living area. Tradewinds from the northeast blew through the house, helped along by large ceiling fans. Sara realized immediately that a talented decorator had been at work here, because the effect was cool, open, gracious, and, judging from the simple opulence of stone, straw, and brilliantly colored linens, very expensive. The Martine house was a perfect example of the ideal combination of taste and money. And Michelle Martine, relaxing on a double wrought-iron chaise longue, was another example.

Mac introduced them, and Sara knew immediately that Mac's twin lacked his warm friendliness. Michelle looked cool too. Where Mac's blond hair was sun-bleached, Michelle's was definitely expensively shop-bleached to a fine shiny platinum. She was fashionably slim, elegant in her bikini, and determinedly languid.

"John Paul," Michelle called imperiously. "Another, please. Would you like a rum and tonic, Miss— Sara, isn't it?"

Sara, still standing, hesitantly said, "No, thank you."

"Sit down, Sara," Mac urged, dropping carelessly on a long curved iron settee opposite Michelle. Sara sat beside him.

John Paul served Michelle's drink. "One for you, sir?" Mac nodded. John Paul hesitated, then suggested to Sara, "We make nice cold lemonade, very fresh."

"Yes, please," said Sara gratefully, with a smile for the solicitous servant. She courteously told Michelle, "You were so kind to invite me for the Christmas holidays. And I'm very grateful for the chance to work with you."

Michelle didn't move a muscle. "Glad to have you," she said lazily. "The more, the merrier." But she didn't sound a bit merry.

"Actually we haven't planned much," Mac said. "We're invited to some cocktail parties and, as always, the New Year's ball. We're going over to the cay for the Christmas luau—always a big bash—yachts from all over the world. And Michelle's opening her shop."

"Tell the truth, Mac," said Michelle tartly. "The reason we come to Camanoe for Christmas is to escape the damned holiday."

Mac frowned at his sister, but tried to explain to Sara. "You know, the rush, cards, decorations, checks for an army of people you've never seen before."

Michelle burst out laughing. "For heaven's sake,

don't apologize!" She said to Sara, "Mac has the world's greatest guilt complex. He wants everybody to love him."

Sara smiled sympathetically at Mac. "It's not such a bad thing."

Mac seemed embarrassed and cheerfully resigned. He asked Sara, "Want to see your room?"

Sara nodded. "Probably I should unpack. And a shower would feel wonderful."

Michelle did not move. Mac led the way along the veranda to the Jasmine bedroom. They stopped to gaze out at the view spread out at a 300° angle many feet below.

"Breathtaking," Sara commented almost in a whisper. "So beautiful that it seems unreal—like a postcard or a painting. The colors of sea, sky, and islands, that fantastic light!"

"You will paint it," Mac said with a smile.

"Yes, yes! Look, there's a ship. Square-rigged, like an old pirate ship."

"You're looking at Privateers' Bay," said Mac. "Great Camanoe was a favorite pirate rendezvous point. Stealing cattle from the little old lady who lived on Beef Island was their favorite pastime—until she invited them all in one day and served 'bush tea'—a deadly concoction that stopped them effectively."

"The islands in the distance, beyond Marina Cay, what are they called?" Sara asked.

"Fallen Jerusalem, and then there's the whole curving chain: Ginger, Cooper, Salt, Peter, and Norman. Tortola is the main island, the largest. In fact, I was headed there when I met you, and I really must pick

18

up some things at Road Town. Would you care to come along or would you rather explore our beach?"

"If you don't mind, I would love to swim," Sara said enthusiastically. "I have never seen such clear water and I can't wait to get into it."

"Best anywhere," Mac declared loyally. "If you promise me that you will stay close to shore and behave yourself, I'll let you stay at the beach while I go to Road Town."

"Perhaps your sister will have some work for me to do?"

"Not today. But don't expect Michelle to join you at the beach. She stays out of the sun—her skin, you know, and her hair."

Sara wondered what Michelle did for amusement. In the rooms she had seen there were no books, not even a magazine, and no signs of hobbies. The large paintings on the white masonry walls seemed to have been carefully chosen by the decorator for their color alone. No music was playing, nor were there any musical instruments in evidence. Certainly there was no TV.

"Where does Michelle do her designing?" asked Sara.

"She has a studio in Road Town," said Mac. "Right now she is resting from her recent labors and sighing for the pleasures of the city. But you will find that she shines by night." He showed Sara her room, coolly attractive, decorated in several shades of pink with white. "Don't worry about the doors and windows having no locks," he said. "Things are safe here. Now I'll leave you to unpack."

"Thank you, Mac—for everything," Sara said,

sounding unusually and wistfully grateful, because she felt that he, not Michelle, would be her only friend in this house. "I won't take long."

Unpacking, Sara tucked the diving gear into a large beach bag, along with suntan lotion, dark glasses, an old hat, and some tennis shoes.

Her clothes—simple sportswear, some sundresses, and a linen dress for the holiday—she hung in the ample closet. When she had all of her belongings nicely stowed away, the closet was not even half full. Most guests, she supposed, brought lots of smart clothing to this house. But she was different: a working guest.

In the shower she found herself singing softly and was rather surprised. Perhaps she would be all right after all on this Christmas vacation. What a place! Imagine actually living here. And Michelle seemed bored by it all.

Sara, who loved Christmas—all of it: the decorations, especially the cards, the baking of Christmas cookies, the smell and feel of the snow in Connecticut, the visiting and gift-giving—tried to understand the feelings of Michelle and Mac. But she simply could not begin to understand anyone who didn't like Christmas.

She dried herself on a huge scarlet velour towel and put on her lime-green bikini. Over this, she wore a long-sleeved cotton shirt in case the sun got too hot.

On the veranda Mac lounged across from Michelle. Both were silent. Sara wondered if they could possibly enjoy each other's company. They didn't seem to, but perhaps theirs was a companionable silence.

"Please tell me when you want me to start work," Sara told Michelle.

Michelle looked faintly disturbed. "Yes, yes, later," she said sharply. "Don't pester."

Mac jumped up. "Let's go," he urged Sara.

Mac stopped to give Captain Hook the word that he was not invited on this trip. They drove down the hill in a cloud of dust, noisily shifting gears on the turns and gathering speed on the downhill dash. Mac parked the Jeep near the jetty.

"Beaches all along here," he told Sara. "Probably the most interesting is that way." He pointed south. "Explore and enjoy. Pick you up in an hour or so. You can always walk home if you get bored."

"Have no fear," Sara assured him and waved as he turned toward the boats.

In an arc of sugar-white sand farther down the beach she put on her fins, rubbed saliva inside her face mask to prevent clouding, and adjusted the snorkel. She ran happily into the water, which was deliciously warm and so pure and translucent, she could have shouted for joy. Sara was standing in waist-deep water when Mac's motorboat swept by. He waved madly, and she returned his greeting in the same way.

Now she settled down for some serious snorkeling. Sunlight penetrated the water right down to the white-sand bottom, and she had no idea how deep it was. She dove beneath the surface and explored the bottom. A crab scuttled away. Then a whole school of tiny minnows swept around her, enveloping her in a cloud of shimmering silver that seemed like silk. She surfaced for air, then dove under again to find six yellow-tailed snappers, who seemed very interested in the newcomer to their kingdom. The fish were spectacularly beautiful and pure with their luminescent white bodies, streamlined with a dashing stripe of cadmium yellow from head to tail. Curious and friendly, the snappers inspected her thoroughly. Sara held out a hand, which disturbed them not at all. How marvelous it was down here! Sara could easily understand how scuba divers might suffer from "rapture of the deep" and never want to leave their watery paradise.

Farther along she saw great growths of coral, which she believed to be staghorn, because the coral resembled the horns of a stag. Flowery clumps grew on the coral, gently waving long fronds in the water. Sara went deeper to inspect them closer. Everything down here in the unreal light seemed like a fairy tale. A bright fish nibbled at coral branches. A parrot fish, she thought. Like the snappers, the fish had no fear of humans.

In her ecstasy at discovering this totally new world, Sara reached out to touch one of the waving fronds of the plants that were everywhere on the coral. A shock of excruciating pain hit her fingers. Her first reaction was to put her feet on the bottom and inspect the source of her pain. She couldn't imagine what had attacked her. When she lowered her legs to touch bottom, it hit her again on her lower leg, the shin, and the knee. Sara cried out in pain and tore her mask from her face. Her fingers looked reddish, and there seeed to be puncture marks of some kind, but she didn't wait to inspect them, because now her leg hurt terribly. She had to get out of the water quickly before whatever had attacked her struck again.

Like a confused sea creature, frantic with pain, beaching itself to die, she flapped awkwardly toward the shore. On the beach she dropped to the hot white sand, tore off her fins, and inspected the damage. She was almost surprised to find her leg there at all. A gash on her shin had begun to ooze blood. Several of the puncture marks were visible on the calf of her leg and around and above the knee. Her eyes began to water and she felt a little faint. The intense stinging sensation around the punctures seemed to be spreading, and her whole leg felt gripped in the agony, as were her fingers. In panic she looked around for help, but she was alone on the beach.

Sara realized that she must find help. Because she had no idea what had attacked her, she did not know what might happen. Already she felt weak and faint, perhaps from shock, or perhaps she was allergic to whatever was causing such discomfort. She must not let herself lose consciousness alone on the beach.

Sara stood up and stepped on something sharp. A moan escaped her at the new attack. But it was only sandspurs. She blindly reached for her tennis shoes and put them on, then limped toward the jetty. Her journey along the sand seemed to take hours. Once there, she saw no one. She groaned aloud in disappointment.

Two gigantic black men, bare to the waist and carrying machetes, stepped from behind the post office. They stared curiously, but did not move toward her.

"Will you please help me?" Sara called.

Immediately they loped to her side.

"What is it?" Sara held out her injured fingers toward them. "It hit me in the leg too, several times," she explained breathlessly.

"Does it hurt very much?" one of the men asked

kindly as he inspected her fingers without touching them.

"Yes! Very much!"

The two men looked down at Sara with concern, then exchanged equally concerned glances with each other.

"What shall I do?" Sara asked frantically.

"Why don't you tell her?" a small voice asked tartly.

Sara looked down. A little brown girl with straggly brown hair and a sandy bikini stood staring demandingly at the two men.

"Kathy," one of the men said apologetically.

They had laid down their machetes and now stared in helpless silence at their tiny tormentor.

"Come on," said the strange child to Sara in a disgusted but firm tone. "I will take you to Louella. She knows what to do for sea urchin stings."

"Is *that* all they are?" said Sara, relieved. "From the way they feel, I thought it was something far worse."

"They're bad enough," the child said matter-of-factly. "But they won't cause you as much trouble as that coral cut."

"Why wouldn't those two men tell me what to do about the stings?" asked Sara curiously.

The little girl giggled. "They were too polite. They wet on them."

"Oh, I see," said Sara, somewhat embarrassed. "Where are you taking me?" Sarah realized that they were on the road leading off to the right of the jetty, the road that ran for miles along the water. She doubted if she could make it.

"Home," said the child. "It's up there." She pointed up the mountain, and Sara, limping along, doubted if she could make that either. But she said nothing, saving her strength for the climb.

Farther along the road the child picked up a small green apple. "See that?" said the child, holding the apple out to Sara. "That's from a machineel tree. Very poisonous. Don't ever even touch one to your lips." The child tossed the fruit toward the water with obvious delight in disposing of the evil thing. "They don't bother me," she said proudly. "I'm not allergic." Then she stared solemnly at Sara. "Somebody ought to tell you the bad things about this island," she pointed out sensibly. "Where are you staying?"

"With the Martines. My name is Sara Ann Williston."

"We know the Martines," said the child.

Sara had an idea from the way she said it that no love was lost between the Martines and this child's family.

"What is your name?" Sara asked.

"Katharine Anne Latham." She glanced up to Sara. "Do you spell yours with an 'E'?"

Amused, Sara shook her head. "No 'E.'"

"Mine has an 'E,'" said the child with obvious pride. Then in the unexpected way of children, she giggled. "We have something in common."

"Why, yes," Sara agreed, "yes, we do." This funny little girl was taking her mind off the pain, and Sara could have hugged her. But there was something else about the child, a wistfulness, a longing that was evident, despite her adultlike attitude—a loneliness, which Sara recognized, because she had felt the same loneliness as a child, and still did. "What shall I call you?" Sara asked with a smile, "Katharine or Anne?"

"Everybody calls me Kathy. Would you be my friend?" she asked in a sudden rush. "I have no friends on this island."

"No friends?" said Sara doubtfully. "A pretty and helpful little girl like you? I can't believe it."

"I don't lie," Kathy said seriously. "Everybody here is old."

"No children anywhere?"

"Not on this island. Sometimes they come to visit, but you can't depend on it."

"No, I suppose not," said Sara thoughtfully. "Tell me, Kathy, how old are you? I must tell you that I am quite old: twenty-one."

Kathy gave a little cackling laugh. "That's not old."

"Not really, perhaps. But I thought you might think it was."

"No, I don't," Kathy said, again with that solemn expression that Sara had a giddy desire to replace with joyous, childish laughter—by taking Kathy to a zoo, a circus, a picnic, anything to erase the child's too serious mien. "I am nine years old," Kathy informed Sara with a little grimace.

From Kathy's size and general appearance Sara might have suspected nine; from her conversation, nineteen. No doubt, behind those watchful brown eyes a good little mind was clicking away.

"My daddy is thirty-five," volunteered the child.

"You live here with your father and mother?"

"Only Daddy. My mother died when I was two. I don't remember her."

Another pain struck Sara, around the heart this time. "I am so sorry," Sara said with utter sincerity. "My mother died too, when I was four."

"Do you remember her?"

"Not enough," replied Sara softly.

"Then we have something else in common," said Kathy. But this time she did not laugh, nor did Sara.

They trudged along in silence, passing one house and now approaching another.

"We're almost there now," Kathy said encouragingly. "Does it still hurt?"

"Yes, but not as much."

"Louella will fix you up fine. She's our cook, and she knows everything about these islands."

"Glad to hear it," said Sara with a sigh. "And I'm also glad we're here."

The Latham house seemed to be slightly smaller than the Martines' with almost the same orientation. But this house looked lived-in. Many books lined one wall of the living room. A radio was playing calypso music. Furnishings were sturdy, island-type wicker and straw. The same easterly tradewinds sent cooling breezes though the house. Big clumpy floral arrangements filled the rooms, unlike the Martines', where the flowers had been most carefully and artistically arranged. Sara noticed all these things as she passed through to the veranda, where she now sat, hurting.

Kathy brought Louella, who carried several items for first aid, including a couple of dark green candles. Sara wondered apprehensively what they were for. Kathy introduced the two women quite properly. Sara again marveled at the child's poise. Louella, a sympathetic black woman in a blue dress and an enveloping white apron, got right to work.

"Land sakes, Miss Sara," she scolded, "don't you know about sea urchins?"

Sara admitted ruefully that she didn't, but said she was learning—the hard way.

Louella tried to reassure her, "This isn't going to hurt much more than it does already."

Louella lit one of the candles and dripped hot wax on each of the puncture wounds. Sara thought anxiously of voodoo. Louella explained that the spines of the sea urchins broke off in the flesh and would dissolve into an infectious powder if not removed. The hot wax hardened them again, and they could be pried out, which Louella proceeded to do. But the little purple marks remained.

Like Kathy, Louella warned about the coral cut, and cleansed it thoroughly, finishing the treatment with an antibiotic ointment. Sara, who had half expected folk remedies, even voodoo, was relieved. She told Louella how wonderful she was. Kathy, watching critically, seemed pleased with Louella's performance and Sara's gratitude.

"Now! The bad part is done," Louella declared, rising creakily from her stooping position. "Now, Miss Sara, you gets your reward for being brave."

Sara didn't feel that she had been very brave. Louella returned with two glasses of fresh orange juice. Kathy smacked her lips.

"We get our oranges from Puerto Rico," said Kathy contentedly. "Could you stay for dinner, Sara? It will be okay."

Louella now offered Sara two aspirins. "Better stay," she advised.

"Thank you, but I must be getting back." Sara suddenly remembered that she had limped off, leaving all of her things on the beach, even her shirt. Now here she was, all glopped up with green wax and a big Band-Aid, and practically naked in her bikini. Now that the pain of the stings was slowly subsiding, her face and body began to sting from something else, undoubtedly sunburn. Her face felt hot, and she touched with dismay the salty disaster of her hair. "Oh, Kathy," Sara moaned, "I am a total mess."

At that moment they heard a car, and it wasn't long before a tall good-looking man burst into the living room. Seeing a familiar figure on the veranda, he dashed out there to pick up his daughter in a great bear hug.

"Daddy! Daddy!" Kathy exclaimed happily as he hugged and kissed her and swung her around, her little bare feet flying wildly in the air.

Then he noticed Sara. His startled eyes met hers, and she prayed that she would sink through the floor.

CHAPTER TWO

Astonished, Kathy's father slowly put her down. He stood looking down at Sara with amazed eyes and a politely impassive expression.

Instinctively Sara saw herself as this man must see her now: a bedraggled sea creature with seaweed hair, covered only with a couple strips of green nylon and many spots of dark green wax: a pitiful specimen.

What she noticed first about him were his eyes, a deep-water blue, like the sea surrounding the islands. He was a big man, well over six feet, lithe and well proportioned. Not quite as athletic-looking or tanned as Mac Martine, but he had a vibrant, healthy appearance, except for darker lines of fatigue under his fantastic eyes. His dark hair curled slightly around the craggy planes of his face, giving him a fierce, dangerous handsomeness. Or was it simply the grim expression that he had when he looked at her that made him seem so threatening?

"Sara, this is my father, Christopher Latham," Kathy said in a small correct voice. "Daddy, this is my friend, Sara Ann Williston."

"Hello, Miss Williston," he said, still with the same shocked expression.

Sara thought that Kathy's father looked hot and tired. He wore the vestiges of a business suit, and his long-sleeved shirt was damp and clung to him. Sara supposed that he had been traveling a long way. Finding such a suspect creature in his house must have been disappointing, to say the least.

"How do you do, Mister Latham," Sara said in a small polite voice.

"Sara's been stung by sea urchins," Kathy told him. "Louella fixed her up."

"Louella's a saint," said Kathy's father. "Are you feeling better now, Miss Williston?"

"Yes, thank you." Sara moved to rise. "I was just saying that I must be going." She gave an involuntary little shiver.

Chris Latham noticed. "And where are you going to, Miss Williston?" he asked kindly.

"To the Martines'. I'm staying there."

"Then I'll drive you," said Chris Latham. "You are in no condition to walk that far."

"I feel much better now," Sara said. "I can make it back. I don't want to trouble you further."

"Nonsense! It's no trouble." In a fatherly tone he ordered, "Get your things."

Sara stared at him uncomfortably. "I—I don't have any things," she stuttered. "Just this," she said miserably, looking down at her damp, sandy bikini.

For the first time Chris Latham smiled. Now his blue eyes looked like warm seawater, thought Sara. "Louella," he called. "Please bring Miss Williston a wrap."

"I'm not cold," Sara protested.

"I think you've had a bit of a shock," Chris Latham said gently. "Please do as I say."

Kathy interrupted enthusiastically, "I asked Sara to stay for dinner."

"No, please, I must get back. As you can see," Sara said, embarrassed. "I have great need of a shower, among other things. And I left my diving gear on the beach. I hope it won't be stolen."

Chris smiled reassuringly. "Don't worry. It won't be. We'll pick up your things on our way to your house."

Louella draped a light terry robe on Sara's shoulders. "You take care of yourself, Miss Sara," she advised.

Sara patted Louella's competent brown hand. "Thank you so much for everything," she said, then glanced over to Kathy. "Thank *you* for saving me," she smiled. "Thank you all!" she finished, meaning Chris Latham too, but somehow she was too shy to look at him.

"I'm coming too," Kathy announced.

"Don't you always?" replied her father with an indulgent smile.

Despite his obvious fatigue Chris Latham looked disturbingly handsome when he smiled, thought Sara. He helped her to the seat beside him in a car that resembled Mac's Jeep.

A small shaggy white dog came racing around the side of the house. Kathy scooped him up.

"Toby!" she crooned. "Where have you been?" She and the dog climbed into the backseat. Chris Latham reached back to pat the dog, who welcomed him joyously. "He's glad you're back from Arabia, Daddy."

Sara could hear in Kathy's voice the unspoken joy that she, too, was very happy that her father had returned. "Mister Latham," Sara began, "I am sorry to trouble you when you have just returned to your family. I know this is the last thing you want to do at this time."

"You are mistaken," Chris Latham said coolly. "I usually do pretty much what I want to do."

After that, not knowing what to think, Sara decided to let it go at that. They passed down the bumpy, rocky road at a steady moderate speed, made the turn onto the main road, and soon arrived at the deserted jetty. Chris drove as far as he could along the beach, then asked Sara how much farther her belongings were. Sara saw nothing on the beach.

"Everything is gone," she said disconsolately. She

had spent quite a bit of her frugal funds for a new face mask, because the old cheap one had leaked. Sara said resignedly, "I was afraid they would be stolen."

Chris asked, "What exactly did you leave?"

"My fins, mask, and snorkel, an old shirt and hat, some suntan lotion."

"They will be found and returned to you," he insisted. "But I hope you have some suntan cream to use immediately. You look as though you need it."

Chris negotiated the turn up to the Martine house with easy competence. The little car, Sara noticed, did not travel very fast, but it climbed hills with a sort of hunger, its vinyl awning bobbing gaily in the breeze. She asked the name of the car.

"A Mini-Moke, made in Australia," Chris replied. "Four-wheel drive, perfect for these islands."

"Here we are," Chris said, leaping out of the car to help Sara. Despite modern custom, she still enjoyed this small male courtesy.

They filed into the Martine house. In the entry hall near the door was Sara's beach bag.

"My gear!" she cried happily and bent to check the contents of the bag. Every single article was intact. She glanced up rather shamefacedly at Chris. "You were right."

He smiled. "Of course. You will learn."

Sara wondered if he meant about the lack of crime on the island or the fact that he was always right. Did he plan to see more of her, then? She couldn't help hoping, but seriously doubted that a man like Chris Latham would have any interest in her.

John Paul appeared. "Evenin', ma'am, sir." He

bowed slightly, and Sara thought again how formal was his mien, and how incongruous were his bare feet and the khaki shorts.

"Where are the Martines?" Chris asked.

"They're gone, sir, long time ago."

"Gone!" Chris exclaimed impatiently. "Where? They have a guest here who has had a pretty rough day. Where are they?"

"Didn't say, sir."

Chris looked baffled. Sara stood uncertainly near her beach bag. "Who brought these things?" she asked John Paul.

"Don't know, ma'am," he replied politely.

"Did Mister Martine bring them back?" Sara wondered if Mac might have returned from Tortola and found her things on the beach. He might even have been frightened, thinking she could have drowned. Perhaps they were out searching for her.

"No, ma'am," John Paul replied positively. Mister Martine, he got back from Road Town, got all spiffed up and went out."

"Typical!" Chris said scornfully.

"Then who found my diving gear, and how did they know where I lived?" Sara asked, mystified.

"The grapevine," Chris said laconically. "They don't use drums around here, but the word passes just as fast." He turned to Sara and inspected her carefully with those electric blue eyes. She felt like a butterfly on a pin, a drooping butterfly. "You had better get cleaned up and come back with us for dinner," he said with an air of resignation. "We'll wait for you."

Sara supposed that he didn't quite know what to do about his unwelcome responsibility. She said with as much dignity as she could manage, looking as she did, "Thank you, Mister Latham, but that won't be necessary. I am perfectly all right now."

Kathy said, frowning, "Daddy, this is Sara's first day on the island, and they didn't even tell her about sea urchins, and now they've gone off and left her without dinner."

"Oh, Kathy," Sara protested with a little laugh, "you're making me sound like 'Poor Pathetic Pearl.'" Sara hugged the little girl. "Thank you, darling, but I am really fine. You have done quite enough for me today. Now run along with your daddy. See you soon."

"Not so fast, young lady," Chris told Sara authoritatively. He sounded to Sara exactly like her father when that moment arrived when he had had enough from her and would tolerate no more nonsense. "You will do as I say," Chris declared in his resonant voice. "Now take your shower and slather yourself with sunburn cream. Soap won't hurt your stings or the cut." He took Kathy's hand. Toby sat waiting. When Sara didn't move, Chris ordered, "Get going. We'll wait on the veranda."

Sara, bowing to the inevitable, picked up her beach bag and glanced toward the veranda, where everyone seemed quite content. John Paul had followed to offer the guests the hospitality of the house.

In her bathroom mirror Sara stared at the apparition. No wonder Chris Latham didn't know what to do with her! A ghastly creature! Her hair, usually a shade of blond somewhere between light brown and gold, hung in salty strings, witchlike. Salt water had evaporated and turned to powdery white patches on her skin, where it wasn't already blotched with red, purple, or green. The blue irises of her eyes were surrounded by bloodshot white. Sand clung to her everywhere, and even her feet in the old tennis shoes looked like those of a street waif. If she hadn't been so shocked at the apperance that she must have presented to Chris Latham, she would have burst out laughing.

As it was, she smiled at her ridiculous image in the mirror, shook her head, sighed, and set to work. Under the shower, as she removed the sand from her hair and body, she began to feel much better. The stings and the cut still hurt, but the real pain had gone. Her sunburn stung after the shower, and the healing sunburn cream that she had thought to bring along for just such an eventuality felt wonderful on her skin. She combed the hopeless hair and tied it back in a high ponytail. There was nothing else to do. But her hair was now clean and fragrant, and the color, though her hair was still wet, was again blond.

The tiny gold loop earrings in her pierced ears seemed to look all right, and she wondered if salt water would hurt them. She found the sleeveless blue cotton dress that matched her eyes. New white sandals added a fresh touch. Sara sighed contentedly. She felt good again.

On the veranda Kathy whistled her approval. "You look like a different girl."

Kathy's father stood and gazed appreciatively at Sara. "Kathy, most definitely, this is not the same girl. This is Aphrodite, risen from the sea."

"Oh, Daddy!" Kathy giggled. She scooped up Toby. "Can we go now? I'm starved."

"You know, I am too," said Sara. "I hope Louella has cooked enough."

"Louella always cooks more than we can possibly eat," said Chris.

Back at the Latham house Louella greeted them with no surprise at Sara's presence, but many compliments on her appearance. "You are feeling much better, Miss Sara," she bubbled. "You look very pretty." She left for the kitchen, chuckling to herself.

While Louella finished dinner preparations, Chris excused himself to "remove civilization from my pores."

Kathy showed Sara around the house. There were three bedrooms and baths, in addition to Chris's master bedroom, where they could hear the sound of a shower.

Kathy said with some reluctance, "Maybe I should get cleaned up too. Will you help me, Sara?"

"Of course."

Kathy headed for her shower, and Sara waited in the child's room, which seemed unusually bare. A few shells and some books filled part of the shelves in one corner, but there were no dolls or stuffed animals. Sara decided that Kathy must feel that she was too old for such things. A picture of her father and a picture of a horse stood on the bedside table.

Sara studied Chris Latham's picture, grateful for the chance. When she looked at him in person, his personality so dominated her and caused such a strange upheaval in her thoughts and emotions that she welcomed this quiet opportunity for a closer inspection. His chin was quite square with the suggestion of a cleft. There was a small mole on his lower left cheek and the dash of a scar on the right side of his chin. Heavy, expressive brows guarded the startling blue eyes. But now his eyes had a most loving expression in them. No wonder Kathy kept this picture beside her bed.

Kathy came out of the bathroom, clean but not completely dry, wearing only white cotton panties. "Daddy's nice, isn't he?" she commented.

Sara quickly replaced the picture on the table, coloring slightly because she had been so engrossed that she hadn't noticed Kathy's arrival. "Yes, he seems quite nice," she agreed.

"That's my horse," said Kathy with equal fervor. "His name is Donny. He had to stay home." She giggled. "He wouldn't fit in the airplane."

Sara smiled. "Sometimes they do, you know. There are planes that carry racehorses from one race to another."

"Donny's not a racehorse. He's a gelding."

"Oh, I see," said Sara, smiling at the child's explanation.

"Will you comb my hair?"

"Certainly. Bring me your brush and comb."

"Will you make it into a ponytail like yours?"

"If I can."

Kathy found her comb, and Sara had some difficulty combing through the tangles. Kathy's hair was somewhat straighter than her father's and not quite as dark. Sara wondered about her mother.

"You don't pull at all," Kathy said contentedly.

"I'm trying not to. There, I think that should do it."

Kathy looked in her mirror, studied her hair for a moment, then declared, "I like it this way."

"Don't you ever wear a ponytail?"

"Sometimes. But Mrs. Schoenfeld pulls, and I just brush. I'm not pretty, so it doesn't matter."

"Wait a minute!" Sara protested. "I don't know who Mrs. whatever-her-name is, but you *are* a pretty girl."

"My nose is too big," said Kathy matter-of-factly.

"Your nose is quite straight," declared Sara positively, "and when you grow up a little more and gain a little weight, it won't seem big at all, maybe not even large enough."

Kathy giggled. "It will be too *little*?"

"Possibly," Sara assured her. "Now get your dress on. Your father will be waiting."

Kathy fingered through quite a few dresses and slacks and blouses, and selected a navy cotton that seemed too short for her long, skinny legs. Kathy said, "This is my favorite."

The dress looked quite worn, and Sara could see many newer, prettier fabrics in the closet. "You have a lot of dresses," she said tactfully.

"Gifts," said Kathy with a grimace. "Daddy has this friend who is a model, and she brings me things. They are always all gunked-up with ruffles. I hate 'em!"

"Kathy!" Chris called from the veranda.

Louella had served cocktails: orange juice for the girls and a very large dry martini for Chris.

"Thank you, Louella," Chris said gratefully. "It's good to be home."

Sara couldn't take her eyes from him. His unruly curls had been nicely tamed, but not too much. His marvelous eyes still had the smudges under them, but his taut expression had relaxed. He gently twirled the ice in his drink and lolled back in what was obviously the master's chair—large and long with wide, simple scroll armrests and a matching ottoman. He wore beige linen slacks and a silky blue shirt.

Chris said, "Nice here, isn't it?"

"Very nice," Sara agreed almost in a whisper.

"Your first day here might have led you to think otherwise," he pointed out.

"It's all right now." Sara glanced toward the water, visible between two tall trees whose great leaves brushed the veranda. "Truthfully, I have never in my whole life seen such a beautiful place."

"You are still very young, Sara," said Chris, sounding worldly and wise. "The world is full of beautiful places."

"But, Daddy," Kathy broke in, "you always said this was the *most* beautiful."

Chris turned to his daughter with a smile. "Did I?" His smile grew wider and became more indulgent, as affectionate as a caress. Sara could almost feel in her own being the intense love that this man had for his little girl. "Then it must be so," said Chris comfortably.

Kathy appeared satisfied. She leaped up from Sara's side and touched one of the large leaves at the edge of the veranda. "See this?" she said to Sara. "This is a papaya, the daddy." She skipped to the other side of the veranda. "And this one is the mommy. You have to have them both, or they don't have any papaya babies."

"Kathy," Chris drawled, "I am sure that Miss Williston does not need a botany lesson on the love life of the papaya."

Sara gave Kathy a warm smile, then turned to her

father. "But I do," she said. "I had no idea that papayas had such requirements."

"Probably we have one or two of the babies in our refrigerator," Chris said. "If you won't feel too cannibalistic, we might let you try one."

With Kathy's sudden departure Toby had jumped into Sara's lap, where he had settled down quite happily while she stroked his silky fur.

"He likes you," Kathy said approvingly. "He doesn't take to everyone."

Louella told them dinner was ready.

At the dining table, which also overlooked the open veranda and shared the fantastic view, two large silver and crystal hurricane lamps shed a soft glow. Chris helped to seat both girls, then seated himself in the enormous wicker peacock chair at the head of the table. Louella had set an attractive casual table with fernery and flowers in greens and pinks.

Kathy said hastily, "I want to say the blessing."

Chris's head jerked toward his daughter. Sara saw a hard expression on his face, especially around his lips, as though he had suddenly gritted his teeth. But he said nothing, and Kathy began her blessing, while Sara wondered what the expression could have meant. Chris seemed so innately kind and especially lenient with the whims of his daughter.

Chris and Sara bowed their heads, and Kathy prayed: "Dear God, bless this house and bless this food, and please help me to be good."

It was a quick little prayer. Kathy lifted her head, beaming. Sara could have sworn that Chris paled under his tan.

Louella served their first course, a delicious cold, creamy curried pea soup, followed by a small white-fish with cucumbers. Then she placed in front of Chris a large silver platter holding a leg of lamb. Still preoccupied, Chris stood to carve the lamb, a task that he performed gravely and efficiently.

Toby sat beside Kathy's chair, polite, but avidly interested in her plate of food. From time to time Kathy would cut a square of lamb and offer it to Toby, who accepted the food carefully with a delicacy that Sara had never seen in dogs. Then he would wait courteously for more.

"Kathy, you are *not* to feed that dog at the table," said her father.

"But, Daddy, he's very polite," Kathy said in a sweet, wheedling voice.

Chris was unimpressed. "I agree with you," he said crisply. "I am not worried about Toby's manners. It is your manners that concern me."

"Oh, Daddy!" complained Kathy mildly, but she stopped feeding Toby.

Otherwise, Chris seemed quiet at dinner, and Sara supposed that he was weary from his trip. She learned that he had been in Saudi Arabia setting up a desalinization plant and that he owned a large international engineering firm and traveled all over the world. No wonder Kathy was lonely with only Louella to keep her company.

After dinner they moved again to the veranda, where Louella served coffee and Kathy's favorite dessert: a homemade chocolate ice cream with rummy raisins.

Kathy told her father exuberantly, "Sara has promised to be my friend."

"It's the least I can do," said Sara. "You saved my life."

"O-oh, I did not," said Kathy, giggling with embarrassment. "Would you like to go swimming with me tomorrow? I can show you where the good spots are."

"Certainly, if there's nothing the Martines have planned for me. After all, Michelle did bring me here to work."

"Don't be too awed by her," Chris warned. "That lady can be a bit overpowering at times." He gazed at Sara speculatively in a way that she didn't particularly like. "I expect that Mac will have quite a few plans for you too."

"What do you mean?" asked Sara.

"Please, Miss Williston, let me explain some other time, if you don't mind."

At one point he had called her Sara. Now he was back to "Miss Williston." Strange man! So nice, and then suddenly so silent and mysterious.

"Let's play Scrabble!" Kathy urged. "I'll get the board."

"You will *not*," said her father. "Miss Williston has had a long, traumatic day, and I must confess that I'm a bit bushed too."

"Your father is right, Kathy," Sara said quickly. "All of you have been very kind to me today, but I do think that it's time I get back to the Martines'."

"Oh, okay, if you say so," Kathy groused exactly like a nine-year-old who had stayed up long past her bedtime.

"Then, we'll be going," said Chris. Kathy started to leave for the car. "Come back here, Miss Latham," he ordered. "You are going to bed—right now." He gave her a pat on her little bottom, shoving her toward the bedroom.

"Oh, Dad-dee," she complained but stomped off toward her room. Then she ran back to Sara. "Remember, you promised! See you at the beach."

"Yes, yes, of course. Good night, Kathy."

Sara stepped into the kitchen to again thank Louella for her kindness and to express her appreciation for the excellent dinner.

Outside, the night felt warm and welcoming. As they drove down the hillside the moon, riding high overhead, bathed flowers and trees in a daylight brightness and created fantastic shadows. At the bend, where the vast expanse of water came into full view, Sara caught her breath in sudden delight. Hills and cones of distant volcanic islands rose out of the sea in a harmonious pattern. Moonlight stretched across the water in a brilliant luminescent path that seemed to unite land and sea.

"Unbelievable!" Sara breathed. "If I could only capture it, the exact feeling—"

"Capture it, Miss Williston?" Chris asked, as though she had said something terrible.

Sara explained, "I paint, or try to."

"Tell me more about yourself, Miss Williston," Chris said politely. "Do you paint realistic palm trees, or the other kind?"

"Mister Latham," said Sara with a hint of laughter in her voice, "how can I talk to you at all when you keep calling me 'Miss Williston'?"

He gave a low chuckle. "Sorry, I didn't realize that I was offending you. You are so young, it seemed—" He hesitated. "I don't know—maybe I'm only getting myself in deeper?"

"Please remember that I am not Kathy's age," said Sara, trying to sound mature. "Truthfully I am twenty-one, a woman."

Chris did not immediately reply. But as they drove slowly along the road beside the glowing water, he said quietly, "Sara, I am quite aware that you are a woman. Truthfully." As they neared the jetty he said, "I didn't mean to sound patronizing. Will you call me Chris?"

"It does seem friendlier," said Sara.

He confided seriously, "Thank you for being Kathy's friend. She needs friends of any age, for this is a rather isolated place."

"Are there no children on these islands?" asked Sara.

They had turned up the hill toward the Martine house before Chris replied. "Kids come and go on the islands. The rich kids go to boarding school abroad. Of course Kathy is getting a good education at home. We live in Bergen County, New Jersey, and she attends a good public school, which I happen to believe is better for her development than a private one. And our housekeeper is very good about entertaining Kathy's friends. The horsey set," he added with a low laugh.

"Kathy showed me Donny's picture," Sara said. "Sounds like a good life for her."

"It is, I think," said Chris, but his voice held some reservations. "Most of the girls have horses. Our place covers eighteen acres, plenty of space for horses and friends. Since her mother died, I have tried very hard to keep things as normal as possible for her."

Sara said wholeheartedly, "I am sure you have done an excellent job."

When they arrived at the Martine house, Chris said, "All the lights are blazing. They must expect you." He leaped out of the car and helped Sara out. "I'll see you inside."

"Good night, Chris," said Sara as they stood at the entry.

He did not reply but pushed open the heavy double door.

"Thank you again," said Sara.

"Maybe I had better come inside and look around," said Chris.

Puzzled, Sara glanced at him with surprise. "If you like, but I'm sure everything is fine." She paused a moment uncertainly, then asked, "Would you like a drink or something?"

"No, thank you, Sara," said Chris with some impatience. "But do me a favor, please, and let me see for myself." His voice had a determined, tightly controlled insistence.

Sara couldn't imagine what was wrong with the man, but she stepped aside, saying, "Do come in."

Mac Martine sat on the veranda. A half-full bottle of rum stood beside him. "Welcome!" he called cheerfully. "Good of you to bring Sara home." Mac smiled broadly beneath his well-groomed mustache. He was dressed in dinner clothes, ruffled shirt and tie, which Sara thought rather formal and stuffy, considering the warmth of the night. "John Paul told me where you were," Mac said to Sara. "Join me. Good to have company."

"Sara's had quite a day," Chris said dryly. "You can't imagine," he added with light sarcasm.

"Oh, I dunno," Mac drawled. "I imagine she went swimming and discovered many glorious creatures in our translucent waters, and then she dined in the home of the most distinguished man on our island."

At first Sara had thought that Mac was drunk. But he enunciated his words clearly and he appeared quite alert, despite his apparent languor. Sara suspected that Mac was actually more intelligent, aware, and involved than he pretended. But she couldn't be sure.

"For your kind words concerning me," Chris said to Mac, "I thank you. But you are quite wrong about Sara. She found glorious sea urchins under our famous waters, and she has about a dozen stings to show for it, thanks to you. Why in hell didn't you tell her about the danger?"

Mac flashed Sara a look of innocent amazement. "Sara, don't you know about sea urchins?"

"I thought they were flowers," she admitted.

"Good God!" Mac struck his head with his fist. "I thought everybody in the world knew about sea urchins."

Sara laughed. "You have a dumb guest, who is very tired and who is now going to take her stings to bed." She turned to Chris. "Thanks again for everything. Tell Kathy I'll see her tomorrow." Sara smiled at Mac. "Good night, Mac. See you tomorrow too."

"Hey, wait!" Mac protested. "Why don't you both stay for a drink?" Sara shook her head and gave him a little wave.

"Thanks, Mac," said Chris. "I think I'll have a brandy. Where's Michelle?"

"*You* should know," Mac replied. "Getting her beauty sleep. What else?"

Sara had caught Mac's words, and she wondered why Chris should know. From the way Mac had said "you" with so much emphasis, she guessed that perhaps she already knew. The most eligible and darkly handsome Chris Latham would be a perfect foil for Michelle's elegant, blond beauty. Sara sighed involuntarily. No use to let herself get interested in Chris. She wouldn't have a chance.

Making short work of her bedtime preparations, Sara opened all of the shutters in the bedroom and bath, and she was almost asleep when she heard voices. They seemed to come from the back patio, and while not really loud, they carried clearly in the quiet tropical night. The men's voices were raised in argument.

Hearing her own name, Sara couldn't help listening. The voices evidently belonged to Chris and Mac. Both sounded angry.

". . . is a young, innocent, unsophisticated girl," she heard Chris say.

So that was how he saw her? His ripe old age of thirty-five wasn't so terribly old, Sara thought resentfully.

"Her father . . . Gwennie asked us to invite her," explained Mac. "Why get on me? I won't eat the girl!"

Sara couldn't hear Chris's reply to that, and she would have liked to. But then she heard some low rustling noises, the starter of the Mini-Moke catching, and she lay there listening to the chugging sounds grow fainter.

CHAPTER THREE

Sara woke to strange sounds. For a moment she was puzzled, then remembered that she was not at home, but on a marvelous island. Tradewinds perfumed her room with a fragrance that she could not guess. Frangipani, perhaps. The clackety sound would be the wind rushing through palm fronds. The hushed, intermittent sound would be the waves breaking against coral far down the hill. Birds, too, created an exotic mélange of sounds.

Unable to resist seeing it all, Sara flung on a light robe over her nightgown and rushed to the balustrade of the balcony outside her room. There was that glorious view of sapphire sea and volcanic islands and a ship with billowing white sails positioned perfectly as though in a well-planned painting.

"O-oh," she moaned softly to herself.

"You like it?" a voice inquired.

Startled, Sara turned to see Mac, standing not far from her, leaning lazily against the balustrade. He wore only faded cut-offs and a short heavy chain around his neck. Sara thought that he looked unusually fit for a man who had been up drinking half the night.

Mac moved slowly toward her, and Sara saw that the chain held a long tooth that looked like a shark's tooth. She wondered if that was the style in the islands this year. Mac smiled in his slow, easy way.

"You look very fresh so early in the morning," he commented, leaning against the balustrade and gazing at her with a friendly, but frankly seductive, attitude.

Sara felt a bit flustered by his undivided attention. "The good view is out there," she said nervously, nodding toward the sea. "I didn't realize that anyone would be up. I haven't even washed my face or combed my hair."

Amused, Mac gave a low chuckle. "Such a good little girl. Always washes her face and combs her hair first thing in the morning."

"First thing," Sara admitted with a flickering smile. "What time is it anyway?"

"Does it matter?"

"No, I suppose not," said Sara, grateful for the fact. "This certainly does beat alarm clocks."

"If you care, it's around eight."

"That's not early at all," said Sara, amazed. "I usually get up at seven."

"And do what?"

"Get ready for school."

"Still go to school, eh?"

"I graduate from college this year. And I have a part-time job in an ad agency."

"We don't know anything about each other, do we?" Mac asked with mild interest.

"No," said Sara, staring at the tooth on the chain.

"Shark's tooth," Mac said and turned to show her a

long scar that slashed across his brown thigh. "He took something from me, and I retaliated."

Sara shuddered slightly. "How awful!"

"At the time," Mac admitted with a shrug. "It happened in Hawaii a long time ago."

"Are there sharks here?" asked Sara anxiously.

"Sharks abound in warm waters," Mac said, quietly amused by her reaction. "And people learn to live with their scars."

From the way he spoke Sara had the idea that he meant more than just the scar caused by the shark.

"I have an idea," Mac said with more enthusiasm than Sara had heard from him up until this time. "Why don't we have some breakfast? After which I'll take you sailing. Then I can show you where the good diving is, and protect you from sharks and sea urchins." He paused. "By the way, Sara, I am truly sorry for not warning you about that danger. Are you okay this morning?"

Sara hadn't even thought about it. She glanced at her fingers, where the purple puncture marks still lingered, and looked down at her leg. Same purple marks, and the coral cut looked red, but all right. She said, "I'm fine."

"Indeed you are," said Mac, reaching for her hand. "John Paul will fix us some breakfast, and we can tell each other the stories of our lives."

"First I must comb my hair," Sara began.

Mac laughed. "No, you don't. You look wonderful just as you are. We're very informal around here."

"But Michelle?"

"Michelle won't be up for hours."

On the veranda, where the Caribbean breezes blew steadily, warm and yet cooling, they drank orange juice and ate John Paul's light scrambled eggs with Danish bacon. Not far from the table was a papaya tree, where a tiny hummingbird with his long beak sucked nectar from yellow blossoms.

"He doesn't care about us at all," marveled Sara.

"You're wrong," Mac said quietly. "He cares very much, but he trusts us. He has no fear."

Sara looked on Mac with new eyes. What a lovely thing to say. She smiled at him warmly, but made no reply because she didn't know exactly how to express herself. She still felt shy with the Martines.

During breakfast Mac gave Sara practical instructions: "Wear your bathing suit, but bring some cover, a jacket and long pants, or you'll get cooked on the water. And don't forget your sunburn ointment. You can borrow a straw hat from Michelle and a pair of the Z-sandals."

Sara looked mystified. "Z-sandals?"

"You'll see. Everybody around here wears them in and out of the water. They're made in France of jelly plastic, with non-slide nobs on the bottom, ugly as sin. But essential."

Sara was watching the hummingbird. He reminded her of Kathy's papaya tree, then Kathy herself. "Oh, Mac!" Sara exclaimed as she recalled her promise to Kathy. "I can't go sailing today. I promised Kathy that I would see her at the beach."

"Kids don't remember," Mac said.

"But they *do*!" Evidently Mac didn't know a thing about children. "Mac, really, let's go sailing another day."

"Nonsense, girl!" he said gruffly. "If you think I plan to devote all my days before Christmas to you, you're badly mistaken."

"Mac, I didn't mean that," Sara protested, embarrassed. "But I can't break my promise to her. I told Kathy that I would be her friend, and she needs friends. I think she badly needs friends who don't break promises. She's a funny little girl."

"She's not the only funny little girl," Mac said indulgently. "So we'll stop by their house before we go sailing, and you can make your apologies."

Sara looked with new interest at this thoughtful, considerate Mac, who was indeed very nice. "All right," she agreed, "but only if it's okay with Kathy."

"Worrywart," he said. "Now get movin'."

Sara rose from the table, started toward her room, then turned back. "What about Michelle? Wouldn't she like to come with us? Or she may have some work for me to do."

Mac flashed her his enigmatic smile. "You still don't understand about Michelle," he said patiently. "Get going now."

Sara felt slightly rebuffed. How could she possibly understand about Michelle when she had scarcely seen the woman? They hadn't exchanged more than three words since Sara had arrived.

Back in her room Sara followed all of Mac's instructions. After slipping into a low-backed one-piece bathing suit, she packed the essentials he had mentioned. She was glad that she had thought to bring comfortable lightweight cotton pants and a matching top. Her bathing suit was bright yellow, the other things, white. All looked quite fresh because they were new; a little too spanking new to be chic, she thought, recalling Mac's cut-offs.

Mac entered without knocking and plopped a large straw hat on her head. "Try these on for size," he said, holding out a pair of the Z-sandals.

"Perfect," she said.

"Keep them. We have tons."

Remembering the way Mac drove, Sara removed the hat and tied a scarf around her hair. Inside Michelle's casual hat was the name of an Italian designer. Sara thought that she would need to be very careful of Michelle's expensive chapeau.

In the courtyard Mac told Captain Hook the sad news that, once more, he had not been invited. Then Mac stowed an ice chest and a wicker picnic hamper, along with their beach gear, in the backseat of the Jeep.

"Hot!" said Sara when her bare legs touched the Jeep's vinyl upholstery.

"Take off your shirt and sit on it," Mac advised.

Sara did as he suggested. She said, "I don't usually go visiting in a skimpy bathing suit."

Mac grinned, his sun-bleached blond hair, mustache, and white teeth gleaming brilliantly in the sunlight. "Pity. You look great, although a trifle overdressed. People around here go everywhere in bikinis."

Even you, thought Sara, for she had noticed that Mac had changed into a black bikini that seemed indecently brief.

As they flew down the hill in Mac's Jeep, Sara called out above the noise of wind and the tires scrunching on shells, "Are all the days as gorgeous as this?"

"In the winter," Mac replied.

Everything seemed to sparkle with a luminosity that Sara could not remember ever having seen before. Even on the most spectacular summer day in Connecticut, colors and textures of foliage and architecture never looked like this. And the ever changing movement and colors of the sea seemed to be a world apart, a fairy-tale place that she had visited before only in her dreams.

Arriving at the Latham house, Mac slammed on the brakes, creating a small sandstorm. Kathy rushed out of the house to greet them.

"Sara! Sara!" she exclaimed joyously. "I knew you would come."

"Hello, Kathy," said Sara, feeling guilty. She ruffled the child's silky brown hair.

Louella stood beside the door. "Are you well now, Miss Sara?"

Sara told Louella gratefully that she was. Kathy took Sarah's hand, leading her to the veranda. "Daddy's still having breakfast," she explained as Chris rose to greet them.

"Morning," he said. "Care for some breakfast?"

"Thank you," Mac said quickly. "We're going sailing."

Kathy flashed Sara a questioning glance, which cut Sara to the quick. She turned eagerly to Mac. "Why don't we take Kathy with us?"

Mac looked startled, but before he could reply, Kathy said, "Daddy! Please, just this once let me go sailing with Sara and Uncle Mac. Please!" She ran to him, grabbing his arm and gazing up at her father with such intense childish desire that Sara felt would, undoubtedly, melt a heart of stone.

Chris looked exactly like a stone image when he said icily, "Kathy does not go sailing."

Mac said nothing. Sara looked to him for help, but he remained carefully impassive.

Bewildered, Sara said, "I'm sorry. I only thought—"

Chris said politely, "I am sure you meant well, Sara. But Kathy and I are going to Road Town today."

"Daddy, are we?" asked Kathy, somewhat mollified. "You didn't tell me."

"I have just decided," Chris said.

Sara thought that remark was unjustified and quite rude and inconsiderate. "I am sorry," Sara explained to Kathy. "But we shall have many days together, and this was one of the few days that Mac could go sailing."

"Is that so?" Chris asked Mac with an ironic smile.

Mac cheerfully ignored the slur. "Well, we had better be off, then, for Blunder Bay."

"Is that really a place?" Sara asked skeptically.

"Near Virgin Gorda," said Kathy.

"Come, Sara," Mac said, taking her hand. "The day will not be long enough to teach you all the things you need to know about these islands."

"And their strange inhabitants," Chris said evenly.

Sara wondered why he was being so deliberately unpleasant today. But Kathy seemed all right, now that she would be with her father. Sara thought that would be good for Kathy, since she evidently saw so little of him.

"Good-bye, dear," she said, kissing the child. "Have fun in Road Town."

Chris stood in the doorway, watching them leave. Sara did not hear him say good-bye.

As Mac made a screeching turn to the left at the bottom of the hill, Sara asked, "Isn't your boat the other way?"

"No, I keep it here at a friend's house. Know anything about sailing?"

"Only as a passenger," Sara admitted. "But I would like to learn."

"Lucky lady!" said Mac, cheerfully immodest. "You will have the best sailor in these waters to teach you."

Sara laughed. "Lucky indeed!"

"Of course I really had planned for you to recline on silk cushions in the bottom of the boat while I gazed on your beauty and dropped cool green grapes into your mouth." He gave her a roguish grin.

They parked at a beach house that seemed deserted. Smaller, less attractive than the Latham and Martine houses, it needed a coat of paint and quite a lot of weeding in the garden. A row of old, bleached seashells lined a windowsill.

"Does your friend still live here?" Sara asked doubtfully.

"Not now. The house belonged to a French photographer that I knew. But it didn't look much better when he was here. He had very little interest in material things." Mac reached up over the door and found a key. "Want to see inside?"

"All right. But I thought doors were never locked on this island."

"Everybody knows where the keys are kept," said Mac. "But it's traditional to lock doors when you leave forever."

"Forever?"

"Yes," said Mac, casting Sara a cool, assessing glance. "My friend committed suicide in Istanbul."

"Oh! I am so sorry," said Sara, wide-eyed.

"No need to be. I'm sure it made him very happy." Mac stood in the center of the large room that seemed to comprise most of the house. He spread his arms wide. "This is all of it, except for the bedroom over there."

Sara glanced around at musty wicker furniture and spiderwebs. Strangely there seemed to be little real dust. Sara didn't want to think about Mac's friend, the photographer, who had lived here. She said uneasily, "Mac, let's get out of here. This place depresses me."

"Your wish is my command, fair lady," said Mac in his usual cheerful manner.

Outside he led her down a flight of concrete steps to the beach. Beside a rotting jetty was a handsome sailboat, about fifteen feet long, Sara guessed. The mainsail was turquoise and white, and the white hull seemed to be floating on air because of the translucent water below.

On the posts of the jetty below the waterline Sara could see pink and white flowery growths. In the shallow water were lavender clumps of coral, and in the deeper water elkhorn and staghorn coral. While Mac was busy stowing their gear, Sara eased herself into the water, avoiding the sea urchins that she now recognized. Gently, she touched one of the pretty pink-tipped flowers waving in the water. It immediately disappeared into a tubelike protuberance.

Astonished, she called out to Mac, "What is it?"

"Sara, you're hopeless," said Mac, exasperated. "That animal that you just touched was a sea anemone. And they sting too. Why must you go around *touching* everything?"

"It didn't sting me."

"Luck of the innocent. Maybe we should get you some white gloves."

Sara laughed. "Am I to go formal to the bottom of the sea?"

"No kidding. Gloves are good around coral. Another thing people do when they're diving, my love, is keep their hands at their sides. It helps a lot."

Sara said impishly, "I'll try to remember."

Mac said, "Get ready to cast off."

He pushed away from the jetty. First he trimmed the jib, then the mainsail. A fair wind caught them, and the little boat welcomed the wind and surged forward, eager as a horse being let out to pasture.

Feeling the exhilaration of wind and salt spray against her face and listening to the lovely swooshing sound of the boat as it slid through the turquoise water, Sara thought suddenly of Chris Latham. What did he have against sailing? Or was it that he didn't trust them with his precious daughter?

From here, as they sailed parallel to Great Camanoe's shoreline, she could see the white roof of the Latham house rising from the surrounding green foliage. Marina Cay was behind them, and a fairly large island loomed to starboard. Mac told her it was called Scrub Island.

Sara felt that Mac was an experienced sailor, for he seemed to feel the moods of the boat, keeping it running free with very little effort on his part. With his blond hair and strong square features, he looked every inch a Viking.

"Happy, Sara?" asked the sailor.

"Very happy." And she was surprised that this was so, for she had expected to be rather unhappy this Christmas holiday. They were silent for several moments, both appreciative. Sara then commented, "Mac, you seem to have such easy control of wind and sea. I'm impressed."

"No person controls the sea," Mac replied with unusual humility. "I am merely cooperating. If I follow the rules, the sea will be kind to me—perhaps. Even if I do everything right, there might come a time when she will clobber me. The sea, Sara, is all-powerful. I have great respect for her."

Now they had entered the channel between Great Camanoe and Scrub Island. Here the waves seemed higher and the wind stronger. Mac thoroughly enjoyed sailing in the heavier seas, but Sara thought that the waves looked rather high for such a small boat. Mac explained that they were on a beat to windward, and all was well.

"Don't look so scared," said Mac. "These waters are the safest in the world. Even an inexperienced sailor can manage in such clear water. Tides only vary about a foot, and there's never any fog. You can easily see the coral heads. See that yellow-brown area with a mottled tinge?"

Sara leaned over the rail and watched the brownish area come closer.

"You can judge by the color of the water," said Mac.

"That's coral at about ten feet. If it was a sandy bottom, the water would be pale green."

"And is the deep water sapphire blue?"

"Right. But it's lighter over sand."

"You *are* teaching me."

"The day is young," Mac said with a grin. "And that reminds me. Night sailing here is out. Besides the danger of the coral, the native boats don't bother with lights."

"There must be a lot of collisions."

"Surprisingly few. Tortolans have a natural feel for these waters." Then he said enthusiastically, "Why don't you stay for a while and really get to know the islands and the people?"

Sara replied fervently, "I would love to, but I'll never graduate if I don't get back. And I hope they will miss me at the agency."

"Maybe you could learn more here than in school," Mac said with a wink. "Michelle might keep you on permanently."

North of Scrub Island, Mac asked Sara if she would like to try sailing the boat. The waters were not as peaceful as she would have preferred, but Sara said she was game to try.

"Sailing is easy," Mac insisted. "Here, take the tiller. All you have to remember is that when you want to go right, or starboard, the tiller goes to the left, port. And vice versa. Keep her in trim, about a forty-five-degree angle from the direction of the wind."

"But Mac!" Sara protested. "How do I know where the wind is?" The boat seemed suddenly sluggish.

"Look and listen. When you see a luff at the top of

the sail, bring her back, like this." He took in the mainsail a bit, and they were again making headway.

"What's a luff?" Sara yelled. "Look! We're tipping!"

Mac righted the boat slightly, laughing. "It's called heeling. This is what makes sailing fun."

"Not for me," said Sara. "Here, the tiller is all yours. Teach me in smoother waters."

"Sure thing, my love," Mac agreed good-naturedly. "Looks like we're getting a taste of the Christmas Winds. And you're getting a lot of sun. What say we find ourselves a nice deserted beach and have lunch?"

"Fine with me," Sara said gratefully. She felt hot and suddenly tired from her short battle with wind and sea. She slipped on her shirt and tied on Michelle's hat.

Mac brought the boat around, and later they sailed into quieter waters, and at last into a pretty little cove with white sand, where they anchored in shallow water. They carried the picnic things ashore, holding everything over their heads.

Sara said, "I feel like Robinson Crusoe."

In the sun-speckled shade of a coconut palm Mac spread a blanket, on which he then spread his sun-browned, athletic body. "And I am Friday," he said comfortably.

Sara stooped to pick up a shell. "Pretty," she declared. "They look as though they've been freshly minted." The island seemed rocky and hilly with some green scrub and, on closer inspection, the sand in the curving cove had a pinkish glow. "The whole island looks brand-new."

Mac said, "I had it made especially for us."

Sara sat down beside him. "You think of everything."

"You can count on it," he assured her. "Now take off Michelle's ridiculous hat, and the shirt too. We're in the shade, where I think you should stay during the next couple of hours."

"Two whole hours?" asked Sara, removing the hat.

"The hottest time of day. The sun here can be very mean to fair-skinned ladies."

"Does this island have a name?"

"It's one of the Dogs."

"You're kidding."

"George Dog, I think. The Dogs are mostly rock."

"How many islands are in the British Virgin Islands?"

"Depends on how you count, whether you count rocks, cays, islets, banks, or real islands."

"Counting everything—"

"Forty, sixty. Who cares? As long as you and I are on *this* island." Mac's fingers gently brushed her thigh.

Sara felt that his touch was merely friendly, but it bothered her a little, and she moved to reach for a shell near the blanket, dislodging Mac's hand. He seemed not to notice. Sara asked with new energy, "Shall we explore the island?"

"You don't listen," Mac complained. "You are to stay out of the sun. How would you like a cold drink and some lunch?"

"Good idea. I'm thirsty."

Mac reached for the cooler. "We just happen to have the remedy for that."

He found the paper cups and poured two glasses of

lemonade from a Thermos. After setting a small ice bucket on the blanket, he then removed a large bottle of rum from the hamper. He opened the rum and began to pour some of the liquor into Sara's cup.

She quickly removed the cup. "No, Mac. I don't drink."

"A little rum never hurt anyone," he said reasonably. "Come on, Sara, you will see. It helps the lemonade."

"No, Mac, please. I can't stand the taste of alcohol."

Mac grinned wickedly. "Aha! You are not as innocent as you seem. You have already sampled the evils of liquor."

"Don't make fun of me," Sara said seriously. "My father, a most progressive man, let me find out for myself before I reached my teens. It didn't take long to convince me that I neither liked, nor wanted, the stuff."

Mac surveyed her with equal gravity. "I understand," he said. But Sara felt that he was treating her as one would a child, and she resented his attitude.

Mac poured a healthy dose of rum into his own cup, but did not bother Sara further. She sipped her lemonade, which tasted stronger than usual, and watched him as he poured more rum into his own drink. Sara noticed that he was adding no lemonade now.

"Let's have lunch," she suggested.

"Hungry?" Mac asked. Obviously he was in no hurry to eat. Sara said that she was and began to set out the food.

John Paul seemed to have outdone himself, for there were dainty ham and chicken sandwiches with the crusts neatly trimmed, a pickled bean salad, a creamy potato salad, tomatoes, and fruit.

"Even linen napkins," said Sara, impressed.

"John Paul knows what I like," said Mac lazily.

Sara had the feeling that Mac had taken many girls on such picnics. And she knew that there were dozens of deserted beaches in these islands. Mac was drinking too much and gazing at her too seriously for comfort.

Hoping to divert his attention, she asked, "And what does Michelle like?"

With an exasperated sigh Mac leaned back on his elbows. "Michelle likes cities and parties; expensive clothes, preferably her own designs; handsome men, preferably rich."

Mac enumerated these things in a slow, rather scornful drawl that bothered Sara. "Surely Michelle enjoys these islands," said Sara, astonished that anyone could find them less than enchanting.

"Islands force people to face themselves. Michelle does not like islands."

"Why does she come here, then?"

"Michelle comes with me," he continued in the same slow manner, "like peaches and cream, two peas in a pod, two survivors on a life raft."

"Yet she is opening her new shop on an island."

"Desperation measure," said Mac. "What's an aging model to do?"

"She is still very beautiful."

"True—with her makeup on." Mac's voice strengthened to certainty. "Michelle is also cruel, self-centered, deceptive, and she can be a very vicious person. So you watch out, little lady, and don't stand between her and something she wants."

Sara wished she had never mentioned Michelle. Michelle had everything. Small chance of keeping her from something she wanted. Sara felt there was nothing she could, or should, say. She gazed at Mac with wonder.

"But she's my sister, and I love her," said Mac, sitting up abruptly to pour more rum into his cup.

"That's better," said Sara, relieved. "I knew you didn't mean what you said."

"Sara, you little innocent! Everything I said about Michelle is true."

"Mac," Sara said softly, laying her hand on his arm as a form of restraint. She felt that he was telling her more than he should, some private family matter that perhaps she, as a stranger, should not know. She didn't want him to feel embarrassed later.

"And here's to me, as bad as I am," said Mac, pouring more rum. Sara noticed that the large bottle, perhaps a quart, was less than one-quarter full.

"Have some lunch, Mac," she suggested again.

Although he had eaten hardly anything, he again refused, and Sara began to repack the hamper.

"Time for a bit of siesta," Mac announced with a broad smile. "Lay your little head right here, my dear." He patted his scarred brown thigh.

"No, thanks," said Sara. "I'm not sleepy."

"Aha!" he said with no malice. "I get it. Well, sleep anywhere you like." He lay back, turned away from her, and curled up with his head resting on his arm.

Sara, thinking a nap might do him good, left him under the palm tree. She walked along the beach, where the warm green-white water briefly hugged her ankles then, receding, polished the sand to a luminous perfection. Many shells that she didn't recognize intrigued her, and she returned to the picnic hamper for a plastic bag to collect them. Mac was snoring lightly, and feeling like a mother who had just put a difficult child down for his nap, she quietly left him.

Avidly she scoured the beach for new treasures. Beneath the translucent water she could see little of interest except sand, sea grass, and a few shells. No point in diving. There were no reefs here. She waded out and found some live shells, but after examining them, she returned them to their element.

Farther along she found a hill and a path of sorts. Following the path, careful of the cacti and underbrush, she arrived at the top and saw craggy rocks beyond, and a large island, which she assumed would be Virgin Gorda. Fat Virgin. Between the islands were great waves that, for a moment, she thought were very wild and beautiful. Here, the wind blew stronger too.

Suddenly she thought of their little sailboat. The sight of the enormous waves no longer seemed thrilling, but downright scary. Sara retraced her steps down the hill as fast as she could, picked up her shells, and ran back to where Mac still slept.

"Mac! Wake up!" Sara shook him, but he didn't respond. "Mac, please, you must get up now." Sara shook him roughly, and he reached for her as though to embrace her. She shook him off, and he opened his eyes.

"Mac, I think we're in trouble. You should see the wind and waves by Virgin Gorda," Sara said breathlessly.

"Figures," he said grumpily. He reached for his shirt

and groaned. "God! My head hurts!" He looked at Sara distastefully. "Well, don't just stand there. Get dressed. We've got to get packing."

Sara put on her sandals and shirt, and they left the beach in a hurry. Whitecaps in the cove grew to giant waves in open water. Mac steered the boat directly downwind, keeping ahead of the great rolling seas behind them. The sails were blown taut, and while they were very beautiful, Sara sensed that there was some danger. Mac paid strict attention, no little quips, and not much enjoyment was evident. Nor did Sara ask any questions, sensing that he had his hands full. No other boats were in sight, and it seemed a long way over deep blue water to Great Camanoe and home port.

Every time their boat sank to the bottom of a trough and a great wall of water surrounded them, Sara thought surely they would capsize. But then as they rode the crest, on top of a blue world, she could see Virgin Gorda and several other islands. Then down again into the spindrift with the hull making painful sounds, halyards whipping, and the mast scrunching into its fittings.

Sara held on tight and called to Mac, "Let me know if I can help."

Mac yelled back, "I'll tell you when."

CHAPTER FOUR

But he didn't tell her when because suddenly, in a split second, the wind changed, and they jibbed. Screaming around them with Fury-like vengeance, the wind caught the mainsail. The metal rod at the stern, by which the sail was trimmed, was ripped out of the boat.

"There goes the traveler," Mac yelled with an incredulous expression engraved on his face.

Sara watched it all happening, as though in slow motion. The port ropes supporting the mast were swept away by the boom, and for a moment the mast seemed to be standing alone. Then, with an agonized groan, it crashed into the water. Only a splintered stump remained. A rumpled mass of turquoise and white Dacron sail lay useless in the water.

Looking to Mac, Sara suppressed with difficulty a desire to ask him what would happen next. With shocked horror she saw that they were being carried away from the nearest shore.

Mac said nothing, but whipped out a knife and began to cut away the canvas. When he had finished, he found two paddles, and handed one to Sara.

"Pull and be damn, m'hearty," he ordered. "If we stay on this tack, we'll end up in England."

Sara did not hesitate and soon caught on to the rhythm of Mac's paddling. At first they seemed to be making little headway. But then the sudden wind gusts died down almost as quickly as they had struck, and Sara noticed that the nearest land seemed closer. The waves, though still too high for Sara's comfort, seemed to be steady and strong in their favor. But she also noticed that the sun was setting rather fast. The sky color had deepened from gold to deep rose.

It was then that she asked where they were.

"Not too far from home," Mac said cheerfully. "We're heading for Scrub."

"Wonderful! That's right across from Camanoe."

"Right! But the swells are taking us into the north side of the island, a little too far for either swimming or paddling home."

Scrub Island appeared to Sara like two great green-brown elongated mountains, rising out of the ink-blue water. She could see a fringe of white edging part of the island, undoubtedly sand beaches. Now the sun was sinking fast and had disappeared over the land-mass to their right, which would certainly be Great Camanoe, and home. So near and yet so far!

As they approached the island Sara asked eagerly. "Why don't we go in here?"

Mac shook his head. "Too much coral. A little bit farther on, and we can take her almost into shore."

When they anchored, Mac warned Sara, "Watch out for your spiny friends."

Fortunately there was still enough light to see the

dark shadows of the sea urchins as they carried their gear ashore.

Onshore they were immediately attacked by sand flies.

Mac grinned at Sara's frantic slapping. "Cheer up! They'll be gone soon."

Sara said resignedly, "That's the first good news I've heard recently."

"Then the mosquitoes come."

"Mac!" she gasped, striking out blindly at him.

He ducked to spread the blanket on the sandy beach. "Wait here. There's some insect repellent in the boat."

Sara had dried herself as best she could, but she felt salty, itchy, and exhausted from their struggle with the sea. Also quite apprehensive, for she saw no boats and it would soon be dark.

Mac returned, and when they were both as dry as possible, they sprayed each other with the mosquito repellent, then put on their damp shirts for further protection. Sara found her comb and tried to make her hair less objectionable.

"What do we do now, O Mighty Sea Captain?" she asked with a rueful little smile.

Mac gazed thoughtfully toward the water and their crippled boat. "Well, now, my lovely first mate," he went on in his usual bantering way, "we gather firewood, and we build ourselves a nice little fire to signal any passersby."

"And who might they be?" Sara wanted to know. "I haven't seen a single boat since we started our ill-fated voyage home. And you said yourself that no one sails at night."

"You never know," Mac said optimistically. "Besides, sailors who are shipwrecked on a desert island always build a fire first thing. It keeps the dangerous animals at bay."

Sara glanced quickly to the hill behind them. "*What* dangerous animals?"

"Wild goats," said Mac, making a fierce face. "Ferocious wild goats—and mongooses."

"Mac, do be serious," said Sara, relieved.

"We could use the fire to cook our dinner," Mac said hopefully. "Maybe, with the lantern shining into the water, I could dive for some lobsters."

"No, Mac," Sara said seriously. "I don't want a gourmet lobster dinner. I want you to stay right here with me."

"Very sweetly said," he said approvingly.

Sara knew that he had deliberately misread her words, but it didn't matter. "Let's get the firewood," she urged. "Then we can have our dinner from the picnic hamper. There's plenty left."

"First, before the cocktail hour ends," said Mac, reaching into the hamper and bringing out the rum bottle, "let us have a little toast to our cozy pied-à-terre." Smiling hospitably, he offered Sara the rum bottle. "Ladies first."

"No, thanks."

"Warm you up," he insisted.

"Thanks, I'm warm enough."

"As you like." Mac tipped the bottle, and when he set it down, there wasn't much left.

"Hadn't we better collect the firewood while it's still light?" Sara suggested sensibly.

"Right!" Mac agreed, tipping the remains of the

rum into his mouth. He tossed the bottle into the brush. "Now, let's see what Scrub has to offer."

Right away they found some driftwood, which, fortunately, was fairly dry. Mac used his knife to cut some shrub branches that he said were candlewood. Making several trips, they found enough firewood to satisfy him. He arranged the wood in a pyramid and reached into his shirt pocket for the matches. Wrapped in oilskin, the matches had remained dry, and the fire soon blazed gloriously with a_reddish flame.

"That's the candlewood," said Mac.

"Now, Sara, if you will please set the table," he said, formal as any butler, "I will find us some soap so that we can wash up properly before dinner."

Mac loped off, back up the hill, and soon returned with some sprigs of a plant. At the water's edge they washed with salt water and the foliage, which had a slightly soapy, detergent effect.

"How do you know all these Mother Earth techniques?" asked Sara, impressed.

Mac grinned and treated her to a fair imitation of Groucho Marx with cigar. "Stick with me, babe," he said with a lecherous leer.

Sara laughed, grateful for his humor.

After they had eaten most of the remains of their picnic, she noticed that Mac carefully laid back a couple of the sandwiches and a piece of fruit. For breakfast? There was still some lemonade, but not much, and Sara would have given anything for a drink of pure cold water. The island seemed quite dry, however, and she doubted if any little bubbling streams existed.

Mac got up to add more firewood, then returned to sit silently beside Sara on the blanket. The bugs seemed to have disappeared. The waves rose and fell more gently, and the sound of surf, now a soft roar, seemed reassuring. Sara looked up, expecting stars in the dark vault of sky, but there were none.

"No stars," she commented. "Do you think it will rain?"

"Let's hope so. We could use fresh water."

"That bad?"

"Not yet, but just in case," Mac said, getting up abruptly. He washed a couple of the plastic bowls in seawater and secured them upright in the sand.

"Surely someone will be looking for us. Won't Michelle be worried when we don't return?"

"Michelle knows my ways," said Mac placidly. "She will think that I have taken you to Virgin Gorda for the night."

"Mac!" Sara exclaimed, blushing, and glad that he couldn't see.

In the silence that followed, Mac added more wood to the fire. "Why don't you rest?" he suggested. "I'll keep the fire going in the best safari tradition." Then he said, lightly teasing, "It will protect you from all the jungle beasts, including me."

"Mac, don't be silly," said Sara seriously. "I trust you."

"That's what I was afraid of," said Mac cheerfully.

Because she was really tired, Sara lay back on the blanket and closed her eyes. Without speaking, Mac removed her sandals and gently covered her feet and ankles with a corner of the blanket. Sara opened her eyes and stared up at Mac and the dark sky beyond his head. She murmured, "Thanks, Mac."

He folded the top corner of the blanket to make her a pillow. "Now go to sleep," he said softly. "Uncle Mac is keeping watch."

Sara woke to men's voices raised in anger. Somewhere she had heard these same voices before. Sara sat up and, sleepily, rubbed her eyes.

". . . foolhardy thing to do," Chris said angrily.

"Can't help it if you're paranoid about sailing," retorted Mac heatedly.

Sara flung the blanket off her legs and rushed to them.

"Behold, your savior!" said Mac sarcastically.

"Chris, how did you find us?"

"It wasn't easy," he replied huskily. Sara recoiled a bit from his angry glower. "We have been searching all the way from Virgin Gorda," he continued roughly. "Any fool knows enough to 'leave word.' "

"A rule of the islands that I forgot to tell you, Sara," said Mac, edgy. "But then you set sail with a most inept sailor."

"Nobody said you weren't a good sailor," Chris snapped back.

"Come along, Sara," said Mac. "Time to return to the glories of civilization."

From Chris's launch they looked back at Mac's battered sailboat, which wobbled helplessly on gently rolling waves. Sara felt a pang of sorrow, as though the boat were a living, gallant person, now sorely wounded. Mac promised that she could be mended. They would leave her anchored there overnight and pick her up in the daylight.

Michelle was aboard Chris's Bertram, an unusually animated Michelle, svelte in white silk pants and shirt. Sara shivered a little in her damp sandy cottons.

"Come below," said Michelle. "We'll get you into some dry clothes."

Sara followed obediently. She welcomed Michelle's sudden kindness. In fact this was the first time that Michelle had shown any interest in her at all. She had thoughtfully brought some of Sara's own clothes. Sara gratefully slipped into her old comfortable jeans and T-shirt.

Topside, Sara noticed that Michelle stood possessively close to Chris as he steered the boat. Now and then she would touch his arm in an easy, personal gesture, giving Sara the idea that Michelle and Chris were old, intimate friends. As Sara had noticed before, they made a handsome couple.

Chris and Michelle had had cocktails, then dinner together. When Mac and Sara had not returned by dark, Michelle told Chris that she thought they might be staying over on Virgin Gorda. But Chris insisted they may have run into trouble. It was he who had instigated the search.

Having scoured the anchorages around Virgin Gorda and asked around, only to hear that no one had seen Mac's sailboat, Chris had become "unduly alarmed"—in Michelle's words.

"Of course I knew Mac would be all right," said Michelle confidently.

"This time you were wrong, sister dear," said Mac with some pleasure. "Not that we were in any real danger. We could easily have survived until morning," he added, giving Chris a hard look.

"Well, I am glad to be rescued," said Sara.

"You were sleeping like a baby," Mac pointed out.

"I'll sleep a lot better in my own bedroom," said Sara. "What time is it anyway?"

"Three in the morning," said Chris.

Sara thought it was a good thing Chris knew these waters too, for she remembered that there were reefs on both sides of the channel between Great Camanoe and Scrub Island, and it was very dark, too dark to see coral heads. But Chris steered with no hesitation, although with his usual care, and they returned to the jetty at a slow, even speed.

The next morning, after Mac had borrowed Chris's boat to pick up and tow his sailboat back home, Sara took her sketchbook to the back patio and began to rough out a painting that she would like to do of Captain Hook on his black iron perch. The parrot posed cooperatively without too many squawks. Bright red hibiscus near the perch added perfect color, and in the distance, through the lush green foliage, Sara caught the glistening slash of deep blue water. In the shade of the banyan tree she felt very contented as she sketched. Intent on her work, she was surprised when Kathy appeared from nowhere.

"Hi, Sara, what are you doing?" asked Kathy, peering over her shoulder.

"Kathy dear, I didn't hear you." Sara gave the child a hug. "What are *you* doing this morning?"

"I was down by the beach, but you weren't there, and after Uncle Mac left, nothing much was happening, so I came up here."

"Have you had breakfast?" Kathy nodded. Sara

wanted to ask about her father, but thought better of it. She and Mac certainly had confirmed the wisdom of his decision not to let Kathy join them in their sailing adventure. Of course they had no way of knowing that the weather would change so suddenly.

"Will you teach me how to paint?" Kathy begged. "My mother was an artist like you. She painted that tiger in our living room."

"Did she?" asked Sara with real interest. "I'm sorry, but I don't believe I noticed it. Next time—"

"Do you want to come and see it now?" asked Kathy eagerly.

Sara slowly shook her head. "No. I don't think so. I don't want to disturb your father. He was up late last night rescuing me, and I don't think he liked it very much. Did he tell you about it?"

Kathy giggled. "Daddy said that he can't understand why your daddy lets you stay with Uncle Mac and Michelle."

"Oh, he did, did he?" Sara felt that now Chris Latham was treating her more like a child than ever. Granted that a fourteen-year difference in ages might be the dividing line between different generations; it was still no reason why the Martines and Chris should treat her as a child.

"Daddy said that they don't care enough about you. He said they are careless with people."

"Well, Kathy, I appreciate your candor in telling me all these things." Sara paused, wondering how to tell the child that she must not repeat *everything* her father said. But Chris was right in a way—she, too, had the feeling that the Martines were careless about people. Yet Mac had a wonderful, innate kindness about him. Michelle, simply, was unfathomable.

Sara turned the page of her sketchbook to a fresh blank page. "Here, Kathy," she said, "take this pencil and draw a picture of Captain Hook."

Kathy said shyly, "I can't draw birds."

"Draw him the way he looks to you. He doesn't even have to look like a bird if you don't want him to."

Kathy sat cross-legged on the patio with the sketchbook on her knees. She drew the circular perch first and then began to sketch in Captain Hook.

"You're doing fine," Sara encouraged. "And he looks very much like the parrot that he is."

A car drove up, and Chris Latham got out. "So there you are, Kathy. Ever think of telling your father where you're off to?"

"Daddy, Sara is teaching me to draw," Kathy said enthusiastically.

"You've been drawing ever since you could hold a pencil," Chris said, and Sara felt the unnecessary cruelty of his words. Why did he dislike her? she wondered.

Then Chris politely said good morning and Sara thanked him again for her rescue.

To Kathy he said, "I must go to Road Town to see Father Gregory. Since his church is having a bazaar and bake sale this afternoon, I thought you might like to come along for some ice cream and cake."

"Okay," said Kathy, quickly putting aside the sketchpad. "Can Sara come too?"

Before Chris could reply, Sara said, "Thank you, Kathy, but I'm sure you and your father—"

"Please join us, Sara," Chris said with a surprisingly

warm smile. "If you don't object to riding in the Whaler. Mac took the Bertram."

"All right," Sara agreed, returning his smile. She wanted to see Road Town, and the church bazaar sounded interesting. Then the real reason for her immediate acceptance came to mind. What she really wanted most of all was to be with Chris Latham. She said hurriedly, "I'll run inside and ask Michelle if it's okay."

"If she's up," Chris said, with a doubtful glance at his watch.

Michelle's bedroom door was still closed, so Sara told John Paul where she was going. Picking up her bag, she glanced in the mirror, then quickly brushed her hair. A sundress and sandals would do for Road Town, she assumed, but she freshened her lipstick.

Chris's boat was open, stripped down for fishing and errand-running on Tortola. It was a sturdy boat with a wide beam that would be perfect for hauling groceries, luggage, and other heavy items from the Beef Island jetty. It had a powerful motor, and soon they landed at the jetty. A cab was waiting. Sara and Kathy climbed into the backseat, while Chris sat up front with the driver, whose name was Desmond.

He and Chris carried on a conversation, which Sara did not understand at all. She looked at the back of the black man's neck, his starched white shirt collar, his neat haircut. He was as tall as Chris, but somewhat more muscular, and he had a soft voice that combined British English with American slang, island patois and a little Old English. Sara wondered how long she would have to listen before she understood the Tortolan language.

From her vantage point in the backseat of the taxi Sara could also study the back of Chris's head. The way his dark hair curled on the neat blue collar of his sport shirt, the broadness of his shoulders, the half-profile of his classic features as he turned his head toward the driver—all these things affected Sara in a very strange way, making her almost breathless, sending a sudden chill through her body; and yet she felt quite warm.

Kathy interrupted Sara's odd preoccupation by saying, "Look, Sara, we're going over the bridge. See, down there is the old bridge."

Sara glanced down. Below, in the channel between Beef Island and Tortola, was an old pontoon raft. Sara looked at Kathy questioningly.

Kathy giggled. She said, "It could only hold one car."

Chris turned around. "An interesting engineering project," he said. "Poles and ropes, and a horde of small boys on both islands, eager to help with the ropes. The boys were the only ones sorry to see it go."

"Big day when Queen came to dedicate the bridge," said Desmond proudly.

"Biggest day ever," Chris agreed. "And I happened to be here at the time—though not especially to see the queen."

"Where was I, Daddy?" Kathy interrupted.

"You know that you weren't with us yet," said Chris. And then, in a subdued tone, "Your mother and I were on our honeymoon." He turned around to the front and was silent.

"Tell us, Daddy," Kathy urged, oblivious of her father's sudden disinterest in his story.

They had crossed the bridge and turned left along a road that took them along the water. Kathy saw green mountains rising to their right and a glorious sapphire bay on their left. Small wooden houses with tin roofs clung to rocks in a most interesting way, and others lined the roadside.

At Kathy's continued urging Chris went on with his story. "For three hundred years the British had owned these islands. But never before had a king or queen visited the British Virgin Islands. You can imagine the turmoil, the preparations that were necessary."

Sara could tell that this was a story that Kathy had heard before, and loved. Kathy listened, rapt, sometimes mouthing a word exactly as Chris spoke it.

He continued, "They began by cleaning up the place. Streets were swept more meticulously than ever. Beaches were raked. New flagpoles and flower boxes sprang up all along the royal route. Gallons of paint in bright colors were splashed on houses and buildings that had always been drab gray."

"Lots of the houses are still the same colors," Kathy added.

"When the great day arrived," Chris said, "February twenty-third, nineteen sixty-six, people poured in from all the islands by plane and boat. Your mother and I were among them."

"But you lived right here on Tortola," said Kathy, sure of her facts.

"Yes, Kathy," Chris replied patiently. "We saw it all, all the formal, proper British colonial proceedings, all the explicit protocol."

"You and Mommy danced at the party," said Kathy,

because Chris had turned around to the front and showed no signs of continuing his story.

"And you saw the queen dedicate the bridge," Kathy continued heartlessly in the innocent manner of children everywhere, "but you didn't care, because then you and Mommy—"

"Kathy," Chris broke in harshly. "I don't believe that Sara and Desmond are too interested in all this. Let's show Sara some of the more fascinating things along the way before we get to Road Town."

Sara wanted to hear more about Chris's early life with his wife. He was right, of course. Now was not the proper time. Perhaps someday when he knew her better—but would that day ever come? Sara fervently hoped so.

"Okay," said Kathy amiably. "This is East End, Sara, where Louella lives." A little farther down the road Kathy said, "Over there is Long Look, where the Quakers lived." She gestured to the right, toward the green mountains. "Daddy, can we visit the village today?"

"Some other time, Kathy. This afternoon I have a definite appointment with Father Gregory. You and Sara can see Road Town and attend the bazaar while I'm busy with him."

The winding road led mostly along the water, and Kathy called out the scenic spots. For Sara it was all as spectacularly scenic as a picture postcard. A few small hotels and quite a few yachts came into view, and then a scattering of small houses before they arrived in Road Town.

Most of the shops, banks, real estate offices, and government buildings were located on the main street.

A huge development, Wickham's Cay, had been built on reclaimed land. Desmond called it progress. But from the way he said the word, Sara wondered if he spoke ironically. Near the center of the town traffic became a problem, with many small cars, careless pedestrians, darting bicycles, and even a few donkeys. A traffic policeman, looking very spanking-fresh British in his shorts, polished belt, pith helmet, and white gloves, directed traffic from a platform in the center of the busy street.

"Can we stop now, Daddy?" asked Kathy excitedly. "There's Little Denmark."

Desmond pulled to the side of the road.

"Shop if you like," said Chris. "Meet me at the church bazaar. Desmond will return for us at five."

Sara loved the town. Bungalows and shops were painted turquoise, yellow, and pink, the exact shades of which she knew that she must set to canvas. Black Tortolan women, beautiful in their serenity, wore brilliantly colored dresses and head scarfs. Children seemed happy and well-fed. Some sold peanuts and candy on the street, but with no real aggression.

Kathy took Sara into a boutique that sold paper flowers and balloons, cards, and plastic funeral wreaths. Kathy said they also had good tuna fish sandwiches, which they had, washed down with Cokes.

Outside again Sara stopped to admire a large purple, Moorish-looking building that stood on a hill above the town. Wreathed in bougainvillea, it was undoubtedly the most outstanding feature of the town.

"The Purple Palace," said Kathy. "It was going to be a fancy hotel, but now it's a plastic surgery clinic."

Sara wanted to stop by the post office to buy some

of the colorful island stamps for her father, who was a collector. Fishes and flowers decorated the stamps, and she bought a good selection. She also mailed her father a letter that she had written while on the plane.

With so many new people and things entering her life, Sara had little time to brood about her father, which was just as well. She really wanted to be more independent, and now that her father was so obviously happy with Gwen, the time had arrived. A man couldn't stay a widower forever, even if he had a loving daughter to care for him. Then her thoughts switched to Chris, whose wife had been dead for seven years. Chris, young and handsome, so obviously virile and eligible. Amazing that he hadn't married!

Kathy mentioned Christmas shopping, and Sara was reminded that she had wanted to pick up something for Kathy and Louella, perhaps for Chris too, if she could think of anything he didn't already have. Mac and Michelle were taken care of with the gifts she had brought along. With Kathy holding her hand so tightly, it would obviously be impossible to shop for her today.

Sara glanced down lovingly at the little girl, who had taken her hand and held it as they walked, exactly as a very young child might have done. In her T-shirt and skimpy shorts Kathy seemed younger than nine, and Sara felt the same melting hurt around her heart as she had when they had first met and Kathy had spoken of her mother's death.

"Let's have some ice cream now," Kathy suggested.

"All right. Where's the church?"

"Back there." Kathy turned around and pointed back toward the center of town.

The church was old, quaint, and had a red tin roof. People milled about the churchyard and sat at card tables eating and chatting. A variety of cakes, cookies, candy, and other homemade items were displayed for sale. Conversations, Sara noticed, were a wonderful collection of calypso and proper British English. Surprisingly there seemed to be few tourists.

Aware that large passenger liners often stopped at Caribbean ports, where hundreds of tourists disembarked and swarmed through local shops like a horde of locusts, Sara asked Kathy if such ships ever stopped at Road Town.

"Not if they have more than two hundred passengers," said Kathy promptly. "There's a law against it."

Kathy continued to amaze Sara. With that statement and the child's absolute confidence about her information, Sara felt both admiration and fear for this little girl. Chris left her alone too much.

"Is this where you go to church, Kathy? Do you know any of the children?"

Kathy shook her head. "I don't go to church here very often. Louella has five kids. I know them, but they live in East End."

"Five! Who takes care of them while she's at work?"

"Maybe her husband," Kathy said doubtfully.

A young black girl brought them ice cream and chocolate cake. "Thank you," they said in unison, and Kathy giggled. She tasted her ice cream and licked her lips appreciatively. "Soursop," declared Kathy.

Shorty before five Chris emerged from the church with Father Gregory, a rather harried, sweet-faced man who appeared to be English. He expressed thanks to Chris for his generous donation to their Christmas fund. Chris explained to Sara that it was customary for the church to hold a Christmas party for local children.

Father Gregory said to Sara, "Mister Latham tells me that you are an artist. Can you by any chance do caricatures?"

"If only I could. But I'm afraid my work is a bit abstract, not so specialized."

"Pity," said Father Gregory. "One year we had an artist who did jolly good caricatures. He was the hit of our bazaar."

Sara felt that she had let down the church. But Father Gregory now seemed to have other things on his mind and was glancing about in an uncertain manner. Chris took the opportunity to say good-bye. Desmond was waiting for them in his taxi.

When Chris and Kathy had delivered Sara back to the Martine house she thanked Chris and told him she had had a lovely afternoon. She thought that he looked more fatigued than ever, and she felt slightly guilty for his having been kept up so late the night before. When Chris lingered at the door, Sara asked if he would like to come in for a drink, but he declined.

Sara said then, "I like your church very much. Thank you for showing it to me. If it's convenient for the Martines, perhaps I could attend Sunday services."

"Perhaps," said Chris, his startling blue eyes fixed on hers as though seeking some elusive answer. Then he said tersely, "I don't go there myself."

Sara felt very uncomfortable under his intense scrutiny. Did he think she was asking for an invitation?

Sara met his eyes honestly, trying to understand the meaning of his odd attitude.

Chris explained matter-of-factly, "I visited Father Gregory today to make arrangements for my wedding."

CHAPTER FIVE

Somehow Sara found herself inside the house. The Martines greeted her from the veranda. Sara saw them in a kind of blur.

"Just in time for the cocktail hour," Mac said brightly.

"Thank you," Sara murmured. "If you will excuse me—I don't feel very well."

She left hastily for her room, where she closed both door and shutters, and sat uncertainly on the bed. Successive waves of nausea attacked her, and she flew to the bathroom.

After the horrible spell of vomiting had ceased, she felt somewhat relieved, but very weak. She returned to her bed to lie down, wondering what on earth had caused her illness. The tuna sandwich? The very sweet cake? The sea or the sun?

There was a discreet knock on her door. "Come in," Sara called unsteadily.

Mac stood there, smiling hesitantly. "Are you all right? We couldn't help hearing."

Sara gave him a wobbly smile in return. "I don't doubt it. Mac, I don't know what's wrong," she said uncertainly. "And I may have to leave you at any moment."

Mac came to her side and gave her arm a little sympathetic squeeze. "Need anybody to hold your head?" He sat down in a wicker chair near the bed. "Can I get you something, or would you rather be alone?"

Sara had known that Mac was a kind, perceptive person, and she felt grateful for him. "Mac, if you don't mind, I usually work out these things alone. Check with me later?"

"Whatever you say, Sara," Mac said, rising. "I'll keep in touch. Michelle is going out for dinner, but I will be here all evening—listening for your call, if you need me."

Sara nodded, feeling another wretched wave of nausea. "Thanks, Mac."

"Shall I leave the door open?" he asked.

"If you like."

He had no sooner gone when Sara again rushed to the bathroom. Would it never stop!

Sara lay on her bed, exhausted, depressed, and, as always at such times, ready to die. Overriding her physical illness was the dreadful, shocking news that Chris Latham was to be married. Shocking, because of the effect it had on her. Shocking, because of its complete surprise, and because she hadn't understood until he had quietly said "my wedding" that she had fallen hopelessly in love with Chris Latham.

Yes, it was undeniably, impossibly true. Impossible, because no one fell in love so quickly, except in movies and bad novels. No one, her intelligence told her, but her emotions denied this. She was suddenly sick again.

Back on the bed, helpless and undoubtedly green, she lay there with her eyes wide open and lost track of time.

Later Michelle appeared at her open door. "Sara darling, how are you?"

Sara turned her head to see Michelle, undoubtedly dressed for dinner, looking absolutely ethereal. Even in her weakened state, Sara's artistic sense appreciated the abstract design of Michelle's long silk chiffon gown, in colors of pale aqua and lavender, and the delicate sparkle of real diamonds hanging from her ears.

With difficulty Sara recalled Michelle's question. She replied untruthfully, "I'm all right."

"You look terrible, darling. Perhaps we should call a doctor," Michelle said sympathetically as she stood near the bed for a closer look at the near-corpse.

"No, these things pass," said Sara. "You look wonderful, Michelle."

"Thank you, darling. I'm having dinner with Chris." She gave Sara another critical stare, barely disguising her distaste. "Well, if you're sure there's nothing I can do."

Stop calling me "darling" when you don't mean it, Sara wanted to say. But she only shook her head against the pillow. "Thanks, Michelle."

From the door Michelle called gaily, "Mac will take excellent care of you, darling. He's very good with this sort of thing."

Sara wished she knew what "this sort of thing" was. All along she had suspected that Michelle and Chris would make a beautiful couple. Now she knew the truth—her intuition had been confirmed.

Sara closed her eyes. Feeling as horrible as she did, her mind began to work again and tell her that she could not simply lie here and die because Chris Latham was going to marry Michelle. People did not die from broken hearts. Nauseated stomachs, perhaps, she thought wretchedly as another wave of upheaval struck. But this time it slowly subsided, and she managed to stay in bed. Mind over matter, she kept repeating to herself.

As her body seemed to respond to the pacifying orders to her brain, she tried to think more intelligently about Chris. Undoubtedly he had known Michelle for some time, and very well, judging from Michelle's attitude. Michelle only seemed really alive when she was with him, which was certainly understandable. Now that she had met Chris Latham, Sara felt the same way.

Sara had always thought that acute unhappiness, such as she was experiencing now, always stemmed from thinking too much of one's self. She must think of other things: Daddy and Gwen. But even that thought no longer hurt as much, and only brought her errant thoughts back to Chris and Michelle. She thought of Kathy then. How would Kathy like Michelle as a stepmother? What would Michelle do to Kathy? That thought only frightened her and made her feel worse, for Michelle could not possibly be good for Kathy. Sara realized that she was being vindictive, prejudiced, and totally unfair, because she didn't really know Michelle at all.

Mac appeared at her door with a white wicker bed tray, elegantly set with a Belleek china tea service. There was tea, toast, and crackers on a pink linen mat and bougainvillea in a tiny crystal vase.

"Mac, how pretty! Did you do this?"

"With my very own capable hands."

Sara said warmly, "You are talented in so many directions."

"Thought you'd never notice. Now do me a favor and try the tea."

Sara did feel better in her middle, but her head still whirled with thoughts of Chris and Michelle, and she seemed to have a slight headache. But she obeyed, and the tea tasted delicious, like Earl Grey. Perhaps she would live after all. The light, crisp oval crackers helped too.

"Now that's better," said Mac. "When the patient takes nourishment, things are looking up." He placed his hand on her forehead. "Not too hot," he declared. "Ole Doc Martine thinks you will live to fight another day."

Mac stayed with her, alternately silent and entertaining. *He really is a darling,* thought Sara gratefully. *If only he were Chris!*

Surprisingly she had fallen asleep and slept through the night. Evidently Mac had removed her shoes and covered her, for she was still in her sundress, now very rumpled. But she felt ever so much better until the crushing thought hit her again: Chris and Michelle.

Under the shower's consoling spray she washed her

hair. Somehow she always felt better with her hair washed. When she had dressed in another of her cotton sundresses, she felt a new surge of energy.

John Paul arrived with her breakfast tray. "Misteh Mac said to bring this," said John Paul with a sunny smile that crinkled his thin face from ear to ear.

"But I feel fine today," Sara protested. Breakfast in bed, unless one happened to be really ill, was unheard of at home.

"Do you want to sit at the table?" inquired John Paul politely.

"Yes, please. Where are the others?"

"They are gone." John Paul's brow wrinkled in concentration. "Misteh Mac said to tell you Christmas is coming soon."

Sara laughed. "I know that—too soon. Did they go shopping in Road Town?"

"Yes." John Paul arranged her breakfast at a table on the veranda.

Another glorious day in the islands. Too beautiful to be sad—about anything. Sara found that she was hungry, even to the point of eating three of John Paul's superbly light orange muffins. From the table she could see two large sailing ships in the Marina Cay anchorage. Looking through the binoculars, she could easily distinguish people on the patio of the hotel and others on the jetty. Brightly striped umbrellas and lounges stood out prominently against white sand, and a few little Sunfish sailboats with blue-and-white-striped sails flitted like butterflies on the shallow waters near the cay.

What fun it would be to sail one of those! Sara wondered how she could get to the cay. Would Chris permit Kathy to go sailing, even in safe, shallow waters? Perhaps they could take Chris's Boston Whaler across the channel to the cay. But then Sara realized that she didn't really know how to operate that boat, and the thought of facing Chris was more than she could bear.

Feeling quite well, and again surprisingly energetic, Sara thought of skin-diving at the beach. But a slight burning on her arms and shoulders reminded her that yesterday had added to her sunburn, and today might better be spent in some shade. She went to her bedroom, applied sunburn cream to all exposed areas, found her old battered painting hat, collected her easel and paints, and proceeded to the patio to work on her painting of Captain Hook.

The bird was gone. Sara looked around the patio, but he was not lurking anywhere nearby. For a moment she considered her next move. Recalling a half-sunken old native boat in shallow water near an abandoned jetty, she decided to try painting that.

She returned to her room and packed her beach bag, including her old Polaroid camera. A cheap, but satisfactory, model that her father had given her, the camera took only black-and-white pictures, but she used it to record subjects that she painted. In case she was unable to return to her model, the picture refreshed her memory, and she could complete her painting.

The walk down to the beach was pleasant. Tradewinds kept her cool, despite the load she carried. Sara passed the main jetty, the shelter, and the post office, seeing not one person. Marina Cay had been bustling with people, but here on Great Camanoe she saw no one.

At the abandoned old boat she snapped pictures

from three different angles. When she had developed and checked all three, she was amazed at how dramatic they looked, even in black and white. In the background was a volcanic cone of an island—she didn't know which one—then the incredible sweep of water. Close up was the boat with a small pilothouse, listing at quite an artistic angle. The picture had a sadness about it, and today she felt in the perfect mood to paint it.

Sara set up her easel and was roughing it out in pastel color when Kathy loped up.

"Hi! Uncle Mac said you were sick. I was coming over to cheer you up." She seemed somewhat disappointed to find Sara healthy.

"Today I'm fine. Where did you see Mac?"

"At the jetty. He was going shopping."

Sara had a terrible urge to ask if Michelle was with him. Somehow she didn't want Michelle to be with Chris. But because Sara was not proud of her jealous thoughts at this moment, she said nothing.

Kathy was looking at the Polaroid pictures. "Not bad," she declared. "Are you a photographer too?"

"Not really. I just take them as part of my painting."

"Daddy is a very good photographer."

Sara was not the least bit surprised. Chris was that kind of man. "Does he take pictures of you?"

"Sure, ever since I was a baby. We've got books and books of me. But he's *really* good. He won a prize at Fort Burt."

Sara asked where Fort Burt was, and Kathy said it was the round building on the point at Road Town. Quite a few art exhibitions were held there.

"Does your father still take lots of artistic photographs?" Sara wondered.

"Not so many," said Kathy, dropping down to the sand. "He is very busy now."

Sara did not doubt that. Weddings took lots of planning. She wondered why Chris had gone to the church alone. Why hadn't he taken Michelle? And when would they be married? In her confusion Sara had not thought to ask, and Chris had not mentioned the exact date.

Looking down at Kathy, serene in her little bikini, Sara unconsciously sighed.

"What's the matter?" asked Kathy, instantly alert. "Are you sick again?"

"No," Sara replied, somewhat embarrassed. She had been wondering how Kathy would take the wedding—and Michelle as a stepmother. Sara asked, "Did *you* feel all right last night?"

"Sure. Did you think it was something we ate?"

Sara said with a smile. "I certainly considered the possibility—all that cake." But actually she knew what had made her ill.

"Louella's husband is sick," said Kathy. "He's in the hospital."

"What happened?"

"He was hurt in an accident at the cement plant, and Louella had to leave." Kathy said dejectedly, "We were going to make Christmas cookies today too."

"Poor Louella. I hope her husband will be all right very soon," said Sara.

Kathy nodded and began to trace circles in the sand. Sara returned to her sketching. This morning the waves broke gently on the sand with a steady, soft sea sound. Now and then a land crab would appear and scuttle away again. A frigate bird wheeled high in the sky. Sara felt as though they were the only two people on the island.

"How many houses are on Great Camanoe?" she asked Kathy. "I never see anyone."

"About fifteen, I guess," Kathy replied. "A lot of the people come after Christmas."

Sara had noticed that the houses were well scattered over the entire island. Each appeared to have its own private jetty. Since the post office, such as it was, stood by the jetty that the Martines and the Lathams used, Sara had expected more activity. Yet she was grateful for the peace.

"Daddy!" cried Kathy suddenly.

Chris Latham, briefcase in hand, coat over his shoulder, strode toward them. Sara's heart gave a lurch.

"Kathy, why can't you stay around the house?" Chris asked with obvious irritation.

Perspiration clung to his brow, and he looked hot and tired. Sara wondered why he couldn't relax. Undoubtedly Michelle kept him busy, she thought enviously. But what did he expect of Kathy? Surely he had no cause to be so curt with the child. Resentfully Sara glanced up at him, and her face must have mirrored her thoughts.

"Good morning, Sara," said Chris politely. "Michelle told me you were ill. I'm glad to see that you're better."

"I'm fine now. Thank you."

"Kathy, I wonder if you can stay with the Martines today. An important client is in San Juan, and if I meet him there today, it will save me a trip to Spain later on."

"Okay, Daddy," said Kathy, unconcerned. Evidently she was accustomed to her father's traveling on the spur of the moment.

"The Martines aren't home," said Sara. "But I have nothing special to do today. I'll be glad to stay with Kathy until you return."

"That is very kind of you, Sara." Chris gazed down at her uncertainly, as though deciding whether she would be the proper companion for his child. "But if I should miss the plane back tonight—"

"Don't worry. I'll stay with her until you get back," Sara assured him. Then with a little grimace: "I am really more responsible than I may have seemed up to now."

"Yes, I suppose so," Chris said cautiously with a slow smile. "Just don't let Mac lead you astray." Then he addressed both of them sternly, "And no sailing."

"No, Daddy," Kathy agreed solemnly. Then a smile dawned on her thin little face. She turned eagerly to Sara, "Can we make Christmas cookies?"

"Don't work Sara to death," said Chris, bending to kiss his daughter.

Chris thanked her again and turned toward the jetty. On his way to Beef Island he waved from the boat as it passed them. Sara felt an ache all around her heart.

"If you don't know how to make cookies," said Kathy helpfully, "I know where Louella keeps the recipe."

"What makes you think I can't cook?" asked Sara with mock censure. "I have been cooking for my father since I was your age. Today, if you want me to, I will teach you all I know about cooking."

"*Will* you, Sara?" Kathy leaped up. "Let's go make the cookies now."

"All right," Sara agreed, reluctantly packing up her painting gear. She decided to take the paints to the Latham house. One day, she knew, she would want to paint Kathy.

Stopping at the post office building near the jetty, Sara left a note in the Martine box, telling them where she would be for the day. Then they walked along the beach road and up the hill to the Latham house, with Kathy chattering all the way.

Inside, Toby greeted them joyously. Sara felt sorry for the lonely little dog.

"Why don't you take him with you to the beach?" Sara asked as she patted the bouncing bundle of white fur.

"He runs away. Toby is a very curious dog, and foolishly brave," said Kathy like a mother talking to the school psychiatrist.

In the living room Kathy pointed out her mother's painting of the tiger in the jungle. The painting reminded Sara of Henri Rousseau's tropical forests, and it had the same imaginative style.

"It's very good," declared Sara.

"Daddy said that the model for the tiger was their old yellow cat, and the jungle was our New Jersey garden."

"Your mother had a wonderful imagination," said Sara.

"Want to see her picture?" Kathy ran to the bookshelves and removed a thick picture album. Sara sat on the sofa beneath the painting while Kathy found the page she wanted. "See, here she is with Daddy."

Sara saw Chris first—a younger, happier Chris, but not as handsome and exciting as he looked today. Chris had his arm around his wife's shoulders. She looked young and rather plain, with light brown hair that was blowing in the wind. Their picture had been snapped on the slanting deck of a large sloop.

"Your mother was very pretty," said Sara.

"Mommy had blue eyes like yours." Kathy quickly turned to another page of the album where a more formal portrait confirmed that Kathy's mother did indeed have wide blue eyes and a lovely smile. Then Kathy showed Sara her mother's wedding picture, a regal young woman in an elegant formal white gown with a long lace-edged train.

"Here's our house," said Kathy, displaying a large rambling two-story colonial mansion surrounded by acres of rolling green lawn. "Nana used to live in this house, but when Daddy got married, she gave him the big house and she built herself a little house."

"Nana is your grandmother, of course."

Kathy nodded. "And she's coming for Christmas."

"That's nice."

"You're all coming too," said Kathy. "It's okay for Uncle Mac to come. But I hate Michelle."

Sara tried to sort out all of Kathy's information. If Kathy really hated her stepmother-to-be, how awful it would be for all of them!

"Hate is a very strong word, Kathy," Sara said gently. "And if someone really hates another person, it usually makes the hater very unhappy. I don't think you really hate Michelle."

Kathy's eyes flashed and she repeated stubbornly, "I hate her, and she hates me too."

"No, I am sure that she doesn't." Sara wondered if Kathy knew about the wedding. Chris had spoken out of Kathy's hearing. But surely he would have told his daughter about something as important to her as his forthcoming marriage. Really, Chris was not a very perceptive father.

Kathy got up hastily and raced over to a corner of the living room near the open veranda. "Our Christmas tree will be here. Daddy has ordered a real one from Canada. We have to go to the airport to pick it up." Kathy giggled, "And we must remember to get Nana too."

"When does your grandmother arrive? There's only today, tomorrow, and the day after that. Then it's Christmas."

Kathy danced around the absent tree. "I know! I know!"

Sara supposed that Kathy did not know the exact arrival time. "Let's get on with the cookies," she suggested, "or we won't have them done by Christmas."

The Latham kitchen was large and well-equipped for an island residence. Evidently the cookies were to be made by a cookie press, for Kathy set out the press and selected her favorite designs: Christmas tree, candy cane, and a camel. She arranged bottles of red and green sugars, confetti, and silvers. Jars of candied cherries and pecans were added to the array before she was satisfied.

Kathy knew exactly what she was doing. "You put half a cherry on these," she explained, "and I'll show you how to decorate the others later. Now we need butter and almond extract—"

"Well, I can see that I'm not really needed here at all," said Sara, wondering who had taught the little girl about baking cookies. "Let me know what I can do to help."

"You can mix," said Kathy graciously.

They mixed, and pressed, decorated, and baked batch after batch of the delicious butter cookies. Decorating them was fun, and Sara realized that without Kathy she would have missed this customary Christmas rite. At the Martine house it was as though Christmas were something to be avoided. Sara wondered if they would even have a tree or make any effort at all to celebrate Christmas.

Three large glass cookie jars held their output of the afternoon. Sara was amazed at how quickly the time had passed. At noon they made peanut butter sandwiches for lunch and had eaten so many of the broken cookies that Sara feared for Kathy's digestion. But the little girl seemed quite healthy and happy.

"Why don't I paint you, Kathy?" suggested Sara with sudden inspiration. "You could put on a blue dress, I think, and sit on the white balustrade with the papaya tree in the background. Toby could sit on your lap, if he'll stay still."

"Yes, yes!" Kathy agreed instantly. "I have a blue dress." She went to put it on.

Sara combed Kathy's unruly chestnut hair, and although it could do with some cutting, she thought it looked very nice framing the child's thin face. Kathy had a pointy chin, giving her face a triangular, almost heart-shaped appearance that, combined with her large solemn brown eyes, presented a most touching picture.

Kathy sat relaxed on the balustrade, and Toby held his head up long enough for Sara to sketch in his face. Then he went to sleep in Kathy's lap, thereby becoming a perfect model. At her easel Sara quickly sketched in the entire portrait in blue pastel and was now attempting to catch Kathy's elusive expression, which was intelligent, rather wistful, and difficult.

Sara hadn't heard the car, but Kathy jumped up and Toby flew from her lap. "Daddy! You're home!"

Sara slowly turned from the easel to see Chris, who appeared exactly the same as when he had left that morning: hot, sweaty, and tired, with his coat slung over his shoulder, briefcase in hand, and his face even more drawn. Kathy clung to his hand and gazed hopefully up at her father, but he scarcely seemed to notice.

"What did you bring me?" Kathy coaxed, demanding his attention. She began searching his coat pockets and found a small package.

"That's not it," Chris said impatiently. "Your present is in my briefcase." Kathy quickly opened his case and found a small Spanish doll.

"Thank you, Daddy, thank you! I'll put her in my room." She raced off.

Chris threw down his coat and approached Sara. Her heart leaped and she was glad that she was sitting down because her whole body seemed suddenly weak. There was a tightness in her throat and a deep amazement that Chris Latham could cause such an upheaval.

He had a strange, serious expression as he gazed down at Sara. He said huskily, "You startled me."

Sara did not understand. "Didn't you expect to find me here? I told you that I would stay with Kathy."

"I know," he said, "but for a moment there you reminded me of someone else." His eyes searched her face for a long moment, then he took a deep breath and said, "I'm sorry, Sara. I know I'm making no sense to you. Please forgive me."

Sara lowered her eyes, overcome by the obvious depth of his emotion, which she did not understand. She asked nervously, "What do you think of your daughter's portrait so far?" Chris directed his attention to the portrait, but did not reply. That, and his nearness, made Sara increasingly anxious. "Just a preliminary outline," she said defensively.

Chris said at last, "I think you must be a very good artist. Have you had any shows that I should know about?"

"Heavens, no!" Sara exclaimed. "I have a long way to go before I get a one-man show, if ever. My commercial sketches would hardly qualify."

"You are too modest, young lady," Chris said kindly.

Sara wished he wouldn't be so patronizing. If only he could see her as a woman, like Michelle.

Then Chris noticed the cookie jars lined up on the long bar that separated the living room from the kitchen. He helped himself to a cookie. "Very good," he declared, grinning like a large schoolboy with his hand in the cookie jar. "You can cook too."

Sara felt the warm glow of her detested blush and wondered if she would ever grow out of the embarrassing habit.

"And how refreshing to see a girl blush in this so-phisticated age!" said Chris with a teasing smile. He helped himself to another cookie. "Spoil my dinner," he said. "Now, if you will excuse me, I am going to get into my chef's clothing and show you that I can cook too. You are staying for dinner."

"But I—" Sara began. Chris had disappeared into his bedroom. Dinner again with just the three of them would be nice. The Martines wouldn't mind, and all too soon she would lose Chris forever. Sara sighed and began to pack up her paints.

Kathy bounced into the room and said that she would set the table for dinner. Sara helped, and soon Chris returned and told them that they could make the salad. In the kitchen the chef and his two assistants worked amicably together, and they soon sat down to a fluffy crab omelet and a green salad.

Kathy began her blessing without prior announce-ment this time, and they quickly bowed their heads. "Bless Sara and Daddy," she finished.

With Kathy's "Amen" Sara glanced at Chris, look-ing for a sign of the strange behavior that he had ex-hibited at their first meal together when Kathy had insisted on saying the blessing. But his handsome, usually taut face now seemed relaxed, and he made no comment.

On this evening Kathy was allowed to get out the Scrabble board, and they played three games, each winning one. Chris let Kathy win, Sara was certain. But she still found Kathy's quick intelligence rather formidable for a nine-year-old.

Bedtime, however, was typical. Kathy begged to stay

up later, and Chris had to firmly remind her that her time had come. Kathy suddenly capitulated and bestowed generous good-night kisses on both.

After Kathy had gone to bed, Chris said impulsively, "Would you do me a very great favor?"

"If I can," Sara said quickly, restraining the urge to say "Anything for you."

Chris asked her to wait on the veranda as he left the room. Sara sat in the peaceful night, listening to the hushed roar of waves striking the coral far below and wondering what on earth he was up to. Being with Chris was both a joy and torture, knowing that soon he would marry and she would never see him again. Sara's good sense told her that she should try very hard not to see him for the remainder of her stay on the island. But she knew that would be impossible.

Chris returned with the small package that Kathy had found in his coat pocket. Inside the wrappings was a black velvet jewel box. When Chris opened the box, Sara saw a most unusual ring.

"What do you think?" asked Chris. "Is it too gaudy?"

Sara was hypnotized by the beauty of the ring, a wide wedding band with alternating marquise diamonds and emeralds. Michelle could not fail to be impressed by such a ring. A lump rose in Sara's throat and tears nudged at her eyes, making it almost impossible to reply to his question.

"Well," Chris urged. "Don't be afraid to tell me the truth."

If only there were some way to tell him the real truth. He was sitting so close to her, holding the ring, that Sara felt overwhelmed and totally enveloped by his disturbing male presence. And the meaning of the ring, destined for Chris's bride-to-be, was causing so much turmoil that she had difficulty controlling her emotions.

At last she managed to murmur, "It's very beautiful."

Chris snapped the box shut. "Thanks, Sara. I liked it, but I wanted a woman's point of view."

In the semidarkness of the veranda Sara was grateful that in his enthusiasm and self-concern he had not noticed the devastation the ring had caused.

CHAPTER SIX

Sara had asked Chris to take her home. He drove expertly down the narrow road that led to the water. As he turned right at the water's edge the sudden expansive view of distant islands and palms silhouetted in moonlight, almost day-bright, evoked a sigh of delight from Sara.

Chris said, "I know exactly how you feel. This turn always makes me feel the same way, although I have been seeing it for years."

"And did that silvery beam on the water always seem to lead directly to you?" asked Sara, overwhelmed by the almost mystical path of moonlight reflected on the quiet water.

"On special nights," Chris said.

"All nights here are special," said Sara.

"Some are more special than others."

Going up the hill to the Martines', Sara was jostled against Chris. Being so close to him on such a glorious night created almost unbearable pleasure and pain.

When they had parked under the banyan tree by the Martine patio, Chris took Sara's hand to help her out. "Sara, you're trembling," he said with concern. "You're not ill again?"

"No, no," she said quickly, embarrassed that he had noticed. "I'm a little chilly."

"On this warm night?" he said doubtfully. "I hope you didn't get too much sun today. For someone as fair-skinned as you, such a reaction is sometimes caused by too much sun."

In the moonlight Chris's face loomed disturbingly close and caused some alarming emotions. Sara knew very well why she trembled, but she could think of no intelligent reply. Chris continued to gaze searchingly into her eyes. Slowly he placed his hands gently on her upper arms, and an uncontrollable shiver flashed through her body.

"Sara," said Chris in a soft, urgent whisper as he drew her closer and bent to kiss her lips.

A tumult of emotions surged through Sara, leaving her dizzy and helpless. Chris led her even closer, and she responded completely. Her entire world revolved on the axis of his lips, and the only reality was the warmth of his embrace.

Then Chris slowly released her, stepping slightly

back, but still gripping her arms in an almost painful grasp that excited her beyond all reason. He looked down at her with a strange, hard expression that Sara could not understand. She stared up at him in total awe.

"Sara—" His voice was a husky, puzzled whisper. "I didn't mean to do that. You must not think—"

Some sense began to slowly seep through Sara's addled brain: a feeling of understanding for this man who was soon to be married, and who in a moment of undoubtedly fatherly sympathy had kissed a young woman who had been kind to his daughter. The day had ended on a pleasant note, and the night was blatantly romantic. Chris was a virile, passionate man. His was a normal reaction, meaning nothing. Sara did not want him to feel embarrassed.

Trying to smile reassuringly, Sara said, "I understand."

"Am I interrupting anything?" called Michelle coolly.

Both Chris and Sara turned with sudden guilt toward the sound. Michelle, in a slim, silvery jump suit, stood in the glow of the patio lamps, dazzling as a shaft of moonlight. As they approached the vision, Sara saw that Michelle smiled in a derisive way, which Sara could readily understand and excuse. If she had found her fiancé kissing another woman only days before their wedding, she would have felt the same way. Sara could think of nothing appropriate to say to Michelle. Even an apology to her hostess seemed inadequate at this moment.

Chris stepped up to Michelle and lightly kissed her

cheek. Sara felt that, under the circumstances, his gesture was woefully inadequate.

Strangly enough, Michelle did not appear to be angry. In fact under her superior smile Michelle seemed quite unruffled by what she had witnessed.

Chris, too, appeared quite cool for one "caught in the act," as the saying goes. "Michelle darling," he said, "I'm surprised you aren't having your beauty sleep at this late hour."

Michelle's smile did not falter. She replied placidly, "I might say the same for you."

"Thanks for letting us have Sara today," said Chris. "She and Kathy had quite a day baking cookies."

Michelle's perfect eyebrows rose slightly, but she said nothing. Sara rather resented the way Chris had spoken, as though explaining to Michelle that she had been no more than a sitter. And then kissing her as he had! Really, he was being rather insulting. Recalling her reaction to his kiss, now that she was somewhat calmer, Sara felt deeply embarrassed. What must he think? He could not have missed her instant emotional reaction to his embrace, a stronger desire than she had ever experienced before. Even thinking about it now made her all trembly inside.

Forcing her mind back to the present, Sara saw Michelle casually showing Chris a very tall century plant that seemed to have been whacked off at the roots. Michelle said, "Tomorrow we'll spray it gold."

"The ubiquitous island Christmas tree," Chris explained to Sara. "Kathy would settle for nothing less than a pine. I'm picking it up tomorrow at the airport."

"Kathy told me," said Sara.

"Well, ladies, I'll be saying good night," said Chris with enviable aplomb. He climbed into the Mini-Moke, waved, and rattled on down the hill.

Sara tried to think of a way to explain her actions to Michelle, to apologize for kissing her fiancé, but she could think of no proper way. And Michelle gave her no opportunity. Switching off the lights, Michelle said good night in her usual offhanded manner, with not a trace of rancor.

In her room Sara was glad that Michelle had decided to treat the embrace lightly. Perhaps it was better that way. Unfortunately Sara could not treat her short stay in the arms of Chris Latham lightly, nor could she forget the urgent pressure of his lips against hers. Her whole body still tingled from his touch. Quickly she made herself ready for bed, then lay there savoring the warm, wonderful feeling. But slowly her emotions quieted, and unfortunately her thoughts stirred with negative feelings. Perhaps the reason Michelle had seemed so undisturbed, and Chris so cool afterward, was that both realized that his kissing Sara had meant nothing.

Sara found that thought horribly disturbing, for she had revealed herself completely to Chris. Now he would have no doubts about the way she felt about him. Sara hated her reaction, but looking back, she realized that there was absolutely nothing she could have done about it. And she realized, too, that she must make it a point to stay well away from Chris Latham in the future.

The next morning dawned, delightful as usual, and Sara realized with dismay that only two days remained before Christmas. Somehow she would have to get into Road Town to pick up a few more presents, especially something for Kathy. Sara permitted herself only one small thought of Chris, who would undoubtedly be going to the airport today and completing his plans for Christmas.

Except for the century plant to be gilded and exhibited as a Christmas tree, Sara had seen no plans made for Christmas in the Martine household. A nostalgic feeling came over her when she thought of her father and all the preparations she usually made for him on Christmas. Now he would be spending a very different kind of holiday with Gwen.

When Sara had dressed and gone out on the veranda, she found Mac, looking freshly scrubbed and enthusiastic as a healthy child, waiting eagerly at the breakfast table. Full of plans for the day, he told her that they would decorate the tree, go shopping, and if there was time, have a sail and a swim. His boat had a new mast, he said, and they would sail her home from East End.

"Fine with me," said Sara, glad to have her day so well arranged. All of her thoughts led painfully either to her father or Chris Latham, and she welcomed the diversion.

Mac, in his innocence about the night before, brought it all back when he said, "Michelle and Chris have taken Kathy to the airport to meet Chris's mother."

Sara did not find his news surprising, only tormenting. "How do we get to Road Town?" she asked, determined to concentrate on practical matters.

"The Marina Cay boat is picking us up at the jetty

at ten." Mac checked his watch. "If you hadn't shown your pretty face soon, I was coming in to get you."

Sara decided to wear her bikini under a tank top and cotton slacks, since they would be sailing back. Adding sunscreen cream and a touch of lipstick, she tied her hair back with a scarf. Her hair had lightened in the sun, becoming blonder as the days went by, but the shade would never be as glamorous as Michelle's carefully colored hair. She had developed a slight tan, although with a pink tone. *Anyway*, she thought, *I look healthy.*

Mac thought she looked wonderful, and said so.

The Marina Cay's Bertram picked them up at the jetty on schedule. Today the waves rose high, the power boat slapped them smartly, and they made the trip in great good humor with three older women tourists who bubbled and giggled all the way at Mac's good-natured banter. Sara thought again how basically kind Mac was, so friendly, so unlike his cool twin sister. Then the picture of Chris and Michelle being wed in the little Road Town church came to mind, and Sara felt miserable again.

Mac, seemingly unaware of Sara's sudden spell of depression, waved an exuberant good-bye to the still ecstatic ladies as they left the Beef Island jetty bound for a day of sight-seeing on Tortola. Mac hailed a taxi, which took them the short distance over the Queen Elizabeth Bridge to East End, where they would check on Mac's boat before they went shopping in Road Town.

At the East End boatyard Mac introduced Sara to several people, all descended from Quakers. Sara, unable to understand everything that was said in the unique British-calypso island lingo, was nevertheless most impressed by the courtesy and personal interest everyone demonstrated. However, their reliability and good intentions did not extend to the completion of Mac's sailboat.

A courteous man named Whittenham explained, "We are waiting for the gooseneck."

A long conversation ensued, with great civility evident on both sides, but still the boat might not be finished that day. The gooseneck was a metal fitting that attached the boom to the mast. Unfortunately this part was still missing.

When they left East End in the taxi for Road Town, Mac explained that the part might have been stolen, but he didn't think so, unless things around Tortola had changed more than he thought in the last few years.

"These are sailing people," Mac explained, "and they're unusually honest, reliable, hardworking folks with great dignity. Perhaps it's a Quaker legacy, because they are quite different from many of the West Indians. They have an odd code of honor: Stealing occurs, maybe oars or a piece of rope, but they will never take anything from a boat that would interfere with its safety."

"And that includes the gooseneck," said Sara, marveling at the ethics.

Mac nodded. "Whittenham said that the boat would take 'just a little minute' more—his way of saying that it could be ready tonight or three days from now."

"Then we'll stop on the way back to check again?"

"Sure. Whit said somebody really 'humbugged' him

up this time." Mac chuckled to himself, evidently untroubled by the inconvenience.

As the taxi climbed the sharp hills on the road to town, Sara felt as though they were on a roller coaster. At certain high points the little car seemed to have sprouted wings, and they took off into the blue like an airplane, only to be jarred back to the harsh reality of the road. Incredible sapphire bays unfolded, one after another, on their left. On their right mountains rose in green-brown splendor. Here and there Sara noticed a narrow road leading up the mountainside.

"Is this the only main road?" she asked. "It's the only one I've seen."

"Like most Caribbean islands there's a shore road and a mountain road," Mac replied. "One day I must show you the whole island. There are orchids and tree ferns on Sage Mountain that are unbelievable. And beaches on the north shore are fantastic."

Sara smiled at his boyish enthusiasm. "I am not sure that I will be here that long."

"Nonsense. You must stay," Mac insisted. "We can see all of Tortola in a day—it's only twelve miles long—and it's the *big* island. If I have my way you will see every island in the B.V.I.—all sixty if we can find them."

"Some I have already seen," said Sara with a wry smile. "With you, if you remember."

"How could I ever forget!" exclaimed Mac with mock ecstasy. He leaned over and kissed the tip of Sara's nose.

"Mac! What will the driver think?" whispered Sara.

"He'll think we're in love," said Mac loudly. "Won't you, Gibson?"

"You are always in love," the black man retorted good-naturedly.

Mac knew everyone. Soon, at the edge of Road Town, they passed a small hotel overgrown with bougainvillea and hibiscus. Mac told Gibson to stop. A sign with fading pink letters identified the hotel: FRANCIE'S.

Beside a small unused pool they had rum coolers. Three other couples sitting beside the pool sipped drinks, then departed at various times and did not return. Something, aside from the derelict appearance of the hotel, disturbed Sara.

Perhaps Mac noticed because he soon suggested that they get on with their shopping in Road Town, which Sara was happy to do.

CHAPTER SEVEN

On the day before Christmas Sara dressed quickly and hurried to the living room, only to find that Mac and Michelle had practically finished their meager Christmas preparations. The tall century plant had been gilded, and on its topmost branch, which almost touched the high-beamed ceiling, was a modern gold and white angel. White paper birds with pleated tails roosted on golden spikes, and there were green velvet ornaments with gold sequins. This was a tree to match the perfect contemporary room. Packages, expertly wrapped in harmonizing colors, lay under the tree.

"What do you think?" Michelle asked proudly.

Sara thought of their tree at home, green and fragrant, loaded with motley ornaments from past years. To her, that was Christmas. "Very attractive," she said in an effort to please Michelle without telling an outright lie. "I have never seen a Christmas tree like that before."

Michelle nodded, pleased.

"What may I do to help?" asked Sara, hoping for something.

"Nothing, dear, thank you," Michelle said airily as Mac strolled in from the patio. "This is the extent of our Christmas preparations." She waved to Mac. "Let's have coffee out here on the veranda while I tell you about our Christmas agenda."

John Paul served coffee, papaya, and tiny pineapple muffins as they lounged in the comfortable chairs.

Beyond, in the Marina Cay harbor, several boats had gathered, two of them quite large schooners.

"Island Christmas," Mac told Sara. "You will meet sailors from all over the world."

"Not sailor-sailors," Michelle explained snobbishly. "Yachtsmen."

Mac groaned.

"Tonight we're invited to a cocktail party on the other side of the island," said Michelle.

Mac made a sour face but said nothing.

"Tomorrow, as you know," continued Michelle, "is

Christmas, and we are to have dinner with the Lathams, an event that usually takes place in the early afternoon."

Sara wondered if anyone on this island ever went to church. After all, Christmas was the birthday celebration for Jesus. Taking Kathy to Christmas services at Father Gregory's little Road Town church would have been enjoyable, thought Sara.

"And tomorrow night," Mac broke in, "we will have a late dinner at Marina Cay. An English-Polynesian luau with dancing under the stars."

Mac leaped to his feet and gave them his version of calypso. Humming and singing his own accompaniment, he caught Sara's hand and led her through a few steps.

"Bravo! Mac," said Michelle with a sigh. "You have to be one of the greatest dancing sailors of all time. Now, why don't you let Sara have some breakfast?"

Mac gave Sara a swift hug and released her. "Merely my excuse to take this pretty thing in my arms," Mac told his sister amicably as he docilely sat down again.

There was a polite knock at the door. Kathy had arrived and rushed eagerly out to the veranda.

"Where are her presents?" Sara quickly asked Mac.

"All wrapped and under the tree," he replied.

"Sara! Sara! Our tree is up," said Kathy ecstatically. Then, remembering her manners, "Good afternoon, Aunt Michelle and Uncle Mac." Kathy rushed on, "Nana helped decorate it, and we made popcorn strings. Want to see?"

"Of course, I do," Sara replied, wondering if Chris was at home. Would she ever stop this ridiculous dreaming about him?

Kathy, eyeing the muffins, was asked if she would like one. John Paul brought milk.

"Santa Claus is coming to our house tonight," said Kathy. " 'Course, I don't really *believe* in Santa."

"You don't!" said Sara, obviously amazed. "Well, I certainly do."

"Oh, Sara!" Kathy giggled.

"So do I," avowed Mac seriously. "At Christmastime he gives us wonderful, fantastic things—sometimes things we never expected in our whole lives."

"Uncle Mac!" protested Kathy, giggling uncontrollably.

Michelle said nothing. For a long moment all of them listened to the child's merriment while they thought their own thoughts.

When Kathy's giggling had subsided, she urged Sara, "Come and see our tree. Daddy went to Road Town, and Nana will get lonely."

With that information Sara thought that she might go over to the Latham house. She had decided on a present for Chris—the portrait of Kathy. But she knew that she couldn't possibly finish it in time. Maybe another couple of hours' work would make it presentable enough for Christmas. Then it could be completed later.

"Kathy, would you mind sitting for me again today so that I could work on your portrait? I was thinking of giving it to your daddy for Christmas."

"Okay," agreed Kathy enthusiastically. "Then you could see the tree and meet Nana."

Mac looked disappointed, but Michelle said, "Run along, Sara. We have no plans for you until tonight."

"I'll give you girls a lift," Mac volunteered.

Captain Hook, squawking excitedly, joined them in the Jeep. Sara thought again what a wonderful Christmas this was turning out to be, despite missing her father and despite her utterly hopeless love for Chris Latham.

Everything on the island looked so pure in the strong sunlight: the sky like blue enamel, studded with puffy luminescent clouds so starkly white that they seemed outlined by a heavenly pen; green mountains; and the sharp demarcation of pristine sails against turquoise seas.

Sara had a sudden, desperate longing to paint it all, to stay long enough to do all the paintings necessary to capture this perfect place before it disappeared. She felt a deep gratitude simply to be here on this day.

Nana was delightful, a peppy, amiable woman with smart-looking short gray hair. Evidently she and Mac were old friends, for they carried on a spirited, reminiscent conversation, while Kathy ran to put on her blue dress and Sara set up her easel.

When Kathy had cornered Toby and brushed him for the occasion, Sara arranged them in the same position on the balustrade near the papaya tree. Mac asked if he could watch Sara paint, and she said that he was welcome to watch, but that he might find it boring. Sara was accustomed to an audience over her shoulder, as she had painted in public places, and a quiet audience did not bother her.

"But you must promise," she warned Mac, "not to criticize or tell me how to mix my paints."

Mac raised his right hand, solemnly swearing that he would abide by the rules. Sara smiled tolerantly, thinking that Mac almost never followed rules. Mrs. Latham excused herself to help Louella in the kitchen.

"At the rate Louella is going," said Kathy's grandmother good-naturedly, "we'll be having Christmas dinner on New Year's."

"Bet your grandmother is a good cook," Sara told Kathy, a statement which brought on another fit of giggling.

"Nana can't cook," declared Kathy between snorts, and Sara had to wait for her to quiet down.

Judging from the way Nana looked and behaved, Sara guessed that Mrs. Latham had no need to cook. Sara thought dreamily that if she were rich, even if she had a very good cook, she would still find it satisfying to cook for those she loved.

The painting was going well. But because Kathy and Toby were unusually restless models on this day before Christmas, they took several breaks. Mac appeared quite at home, making several trips to the bar to replenish either rum or ice, and teasing Sara and Kathy between sittings.

The magnificent pine tree was alternately admired and criticized. Because the fragrant green tree reminded Sara of home, she loved it and said so. Mac moved an ornament here and there, Kathy rearranged popcorn garlands, and Nana brought forth more gaily wrapped presents to add to the bounty under the tree.

It was late afternoon when Kathy, from her perch on the balustrade, saw a familiar car on the road below. "Daddy's coming!" she cried happily.

Realizing that the painting session had ended for the day, Sara put down her brush. With the anticipation of Chris's arrival her heart began to beat faster, her hands trembled, and there was absolutely nothing she could do about it.

Chris entered his house with his coat on his arm, gave one frowning look around and remarked, "What a cozy holiday scene."

"No need to be so grumpy," said Mrs. Latham.

Kathy rushed to her father, but he brushed her off. He glanced with glacial disdain at Sara and Mac, who was helping her pack up her painting gear. "Please excuse me, won't you?" said Chris. "I seem to have another party to get ready for."

"We really must be going," said Sara hastily. Chris's unfriendly behavior disturbed and irritated her. "Mac, watch that canvas, please. It's still wet."

"Trust me," said Mac sweetly.

Chris shot Mac a withering glance as he left the room.

Sara told Mrs. Latham good-bye and stooped to kiss Kathy. "Merry Christmas, darling."

Back at the Martine house Michelle had begun to dress for the cocktail party. Sara and Mac were chatting comfortably on the veranda when Michelle rushed out.

"Hurry!" she urged nervously. "We're a half hour late already."

"Not going," said Mac equably.

"Don't be silly. You love parties."

"Tonight is different."

"How different?" challenged Michelle.

Christmas Eve, thought Sara.

"Sara doesn't want to go either, do you, Sara?"

Sara looked to Michelle. "I am your guest."

Michelle glared at Mac.

"Don't go, Sara," warned Mac with an exaggerated air of mystery. "You'll be sorry."

"Do as you like," Michelle snapped to Sara. "As for you, my charming brother, your presence will be sorely missed. But not by me, and certainly not by the hostess, who. . . ."

Sara felt that she had no part in the family power struggle. Cocktail parties weren't exactly her thing either, since she hardly drank. She excused herself to put away her paints and clean her brushes.

When she returned, Mac was sitting alone on the veranda. "You don't mind, do you?" he asked, peering carefully into her face for her reaction. "It's only one of your usual island parties, British and Americans, a few old residents, meeting once or twice a year, drinking too much and mouthing inanities."

Sara said tentatively, "I like meeting new people."

"These are *old* people," Mac said with careless scorn. "Besides, you can meet most of them tomorrow at the cay party."

"Michelle went on to the cocktail party?"

"A dyed-in-the-wool social butterfly," Mac said lightly, waving his arms in a parody of flight.

Sara said she would like to clean up before dinner. After she had washed and dried her hair and combed it up into a neat ponytail, she put on a comfortable blue and white cotton sheath, sandals, and hoop earrings. Her complexion was tanning at last, and she liked the contrast against the white dress. Each day seemed to lighten the color of her hair. This was the first Christmas, she realized, that she had ever looked so summery.

Mac had changed too, and his navy and white casual clothing gave him a crisp, clean elegance. Sara thought that he looked like one of the distinguished men with perfect hair, teeth, and mustache who lounged on boat decks, slickly advertising one of the Scotches.

Dining much later, Sara thought how strange it was to be here alone with Mac on Christmas Eve, on this candlelit veranda brushed by tradewinds, eating *canard aux pêches*. Mac had made the sauce, flaming the duck and peaches with a practiced hand. Then, sheepishly, he said that all poor cooks burned the food in this way to impress the diner. "Flair, not food, is what people remember," he declared.

Sara knew that she would remember everything. During dinner they could see the decorations of the boats in the Marina Cay harbor. Strings of lights outlined the riggings, making the huge boats seem like glittering toys. A Christmas tree stood on the bow of one boat. Others had trees and twinkling lights, as did the A-frame houses on the cay. Tiki torches illuminated the beach.

After dinner they watched the moon traverse the velvety blue vault overhead.

Mac said seriously, "Sara, this is one Christmas when I feel that I've been given a very special present, one that I didn't really ask for because long ago I gave up even the idea that it might be possible."

Sara listened with interest, wondering what he meant. In the moonlight the perfection of Mac's features, his new serious intent, created a dazzling hypnotic effect.

"Undoubtedly you have been puzzled by the lack of Christmas preparations in the Martine house," said Mac. "I sense a sentimental streak in you, Sara. Now I don't want your sympathy, but I want you to know the truth. On Christmas Day, when I was ten years old, my mother shut herself in the garage and left the motor running in her Porsche. I think my father's infidelity had something to do with it. But kids never know for sure—they think maybe it was something they did. Ever since, Michelle and I try our best to avoid Christmas."

Utterly shocked, Sara could only stare at him for a long moment. A sudden mist of tears clouded her vision, and she reached over to touch Mac's hand.

"No, no. Please, Sara." He patted her hand briefly. "Wait here—I'll be right back."

While Sara waited, she recalled Gwen's words about the Martine family: Grandfather, founder of the dynasty; father, devoted hedonist, but still incapable of denting the huge fortune; one son killed in Vietnam; Michelle, the fine-featured partician model-turned-designer; Mac. Gwen had not mentioned any of the father's wives.

When Mac returned, he gave Sara a small silver-wrapped gift. "Present time."

"Now?" Sara held the gift uncertainly. "But your gift is—"

"Never mind mine," Mac broke in. "Please open this now."

Sara smiled at his obvious eagerness and began to unwrap the package. Inside was a neat box and inside that a velvet box, and inside that—a very elegant diamond ring.

"Mac!" cried Sara, amazed. "Is this for me?"

Amused, Mac replied, "Now, who else would it be for?"

Sara stared at the ring, entranced. "What a beautiful ring," she whispered, "but I couldn't possibly—"

Mac said swiftly, "It's an engagement ring."

Sara couldn't believe her ears. Impossible! They had just met; Mac was older; he had known many women—rich, sophisticated women like his sister. He was out of his mind!

"Mac," Sara began, finding the words difficult to express, "you're not asking me to *marry* you?"

"Do you find the idea so incredible?" When Sara made no reply, he murmured apologetically, "First time I ever played this gig—got close one time, but this is the first—" He hesitated, embarrassed. "Not doing too well, am I?"

"You are doing beautifully. I'm the one who's at a loss." Sara drew a long, deep, shuddering breath. "Mac, you don't know what you're doing. We haven't known each other—"

"No, Sara, please." Mac touched her arm in an effort to keep her from saying the words. "I love you, everything about you," he said with sudden clarity and absolute conviction. "I know who you are and what you are—all I ever need to know."

"Mac," Sara protested softly with a shy, disbelieving smile.

"Sara, your smile is like no other," Mac said in a husky whisper. Slowly he drew her to him.

Mac's arms were strong and warm. He held her firmly, but with tenderness, almost reverently. And his kiss was warm and deep and good. But he wasn't

126

Chris, and Sara felt nothing beyond the warmth and goodness of his embrace.

When he released her, Mac said tremulously, "You wouldn't have to love me right away."

He knows, thought Sara. She had never been good at masking her emotions. "Mac, you are a wonderful person," she began.

"Don't say no. Please, Sara, not right away. Think about it for a while." Mac held her hand now, as though to prevent her from making a decision at this moment. He would not rush her into anything. Mac said, "At first I wondered why I wanted to tell you about me, about our family. And then it came to me that I wanted you to know everything, the truth, so that you would know what you were getting into. I knew that I wanted you to be my wife." He gave her a shadow of his usual grin. "You see, Sara, in my own way I'm a bit of a romantic too. It's all so simple, really. I want to marry the woman I love."

Sara shook her head helplessly. "But how can you be so sure in such a short time?"

"If I said 'Experience,' you would hate me," said Mac with the thinnest of smiles. "But believe me, I know."

Sara still held the ring. She had not taken it from the box, where it glittered seductively. Sara said wistfully, "I could never marry for any reason except love."

"Am I so unlovable?" Mac asked with his good-boy smile, and Sara's heart melted.

"Everyone loves you."

"One person is all I'm asking for," Mac replied. "Wear the ring, Sara. Be engaged to me."

Mac's attractive offer a year ago might have swept her off her feet. But now, because of Chris, even though he would be married, Sara knew that she could not accept Mac's ring. She said painfully, "I can't."

"Sara, believe me, you are the first girl I have ever been sure about. And I'm not just moon-mad either," he said seriously. "I have seen you with Kathy, and I know you would be not only a wonderful wife, but a great mother too. Sara, you are the only woman for me, ever."

Mac gazed at her with such tenderness and Sara felt his love and sincerity so strongly that she could hardly refuse his plea. After all, Chris would never be her husband. And if she married Mac, she probably would get to see Chris. As Michelle's husband. A sudden chill swept through her, and she knew she dare not subject herself to such torture.

"You must accept my ring," Mac went on. "If I don't stake my claim now, I know that I'll lose you to another. But I promise you that none will love you and take better care of you now and in all the days to come."

"Mac, you are a dear person, and I am grateful for everything," said Sara softly. "But you would not want me to accept if I loved someone else."

"Do you?"

Sara had to lower her eyes from his clear, demanding gaze. How could she answer that question?

"Wear the ring on your right hand," said Mac in desperation. "It's a Christmas gift." He removed the ring from the box. "Do you like it?" he asked eagerly, turning the ring so that the large center diamond flashed fire.

"Very nice," agreed Sara.

"Can't take it back," Mac declared, slipping the diamond onto the fourth finger of her right hand. "There! Looks okay, doesn't it? Wear it there until it's time to switch. You say when."

CHAPTER EIGHT

Aware of the tragedy that had happened to Mac and Michelle on a long-ago Christmas, Sara could not bring herself to say Merry Christmas.

That morning she said to Michelle, "A beautiful Christmas Day."

"Isn't it?" agreed Michelle. "Mac is out sailing already."

"But aren't we due at the Lathams'?"

"Plenty of time," said Michelle airily. "Mac left early. Said he couldn't sleep. Together, we watched the sun come up." Michelle added flatly. "Christmas is not our best time."

"Did he tell you about last night?" asked Sara cautiously. How she wished that she could have said yes to Mac! It would have simplified so many things.

"He's not a bad catch, you know," said Michelle with a taunting smile.

"But I don't love him," Sara murmured in her own

defense. "It's too soon. We hardly know each other." But even as she said the words Sara realized how feeble were her excuses. If Chris Latham had proposed, she would have accepted him in an instant.

"If you're worried about me," said Michelle, eyeing Sara guardedly, "Mac and I are twins, but we're not joined at the hips. In New York we have our own apartments. Our lives are quite separate. And I *am* being married." Sara was painfully aware of this fact. Michelle continued confidently, "You would have a good life with Mac. He can afford it. He tells me that he truly loves you and he's ready to settle down at last." Michelle gave Sara a funny little smile. "Under that casual exterior Mac is deeply idealistic. All these years he's been waiting for the perfect mate." Michelle paused in wonder, then said with a certain puzzled awe, "It's *you*, Sara."

Sara felt overwhelmed by the responsibility: Mac's proposal, now Michelle's fervent plea for her brother. Sara felt almost guilty refusing.

Although it was practically noon, they still lounged in their housecoats, drinking orange juice and coffee. Sara said suddenly, "All of this is so strange. Do people change the entire course of their lives so quickly? Michelle, I don't even know what Mac does—except for sailing boats."

"Mac has a business degree from Harvard," said Michelle. "And an office in New York, the family business, which is steel. Grandfather provided so well that not much effort is required to further the family fortunes. Our father, certainly, excelled as a dilettante. But Mac is more serious, despite what you may think."

"Please," begged Sara, embarrassed, "I wasn't asking

for a Dun and Bradstreet report. As long as two people love each other, none of that matters."

"Now you betray your age," said Michelle tolerantly. "It matters, sometimes, more than love."

"Not for me," declared Sara confidently.

Michelle nodded soberly. "Then, for you, Sara darling, I hope it never changes. If it matters to you, I would love to have you for a sister-in-law."

"Thank you, Michelle. Really, I do care for Mac."

"But not to the extent of wearing his ring?" Michelle observed with a poignant glance at Sara's bare fingers.

"That ring frightens me," Sara admitted. "It's so grand, so unlike anything I have ever owned. Michelle, I don't see how I can accept it, much less wear it—even on my right hand."

Michelle sighed with resignation. "Sara, don't even think about the value of the ring. Mac has spent much more for less reason. Do us both a favor and wear the ring. Today, anyway, for Mac's sake. He's feeling rather depressed. Christmas is a bad time for both of us."

Sara nodded understandingly. "All right." She checked her watch. "Shouldn't Mac be back by now? And isn't it time we got dressed?"

"Past time."

"What shall I wear?" asked Sara, wondering if her good jade linen would be good enough.

"Something casual," said Michelle. They agreed on short afternoon dresses. "Your last day of play, my girl," Michelle promised. "The style show and the opening of my shop will keep us hopping after Christmas."

"Good. That's what I want," replied Sara, who hoped that work might divert her mind from Chris.

Then she remembered the present for him. But the canvas simply was not ready to be presented. Instead she quickly made a drawing of the painting, decorated it with a few flowers and scrolls, and wrote Chris a note saying that the oil portrait would follow at a later date. Kathy's gift, easel and paint, were already wrapped. Sara had selected a bright pink scarf for Louella and a handmade bag from the church bazaar for Mrs. Latham.

Michelle presented Sara with her Christmas gift, a frilly long white eyelet housecoat, which fit perfectly. Sara was overcome with gratitude. Michelle said wisely, "When Mac sees you in this, he'll never let you get away."

Michelle accepted Sara's gift of the designer silk scarf and assured Sara that Mac would love the nautical clock. When he had not returned by one o'clock, Michelle thought that they should go on to the Lathams'.

Kathy rushed out to greet them. She was wearing a long cranberry velvet dress with tiny puffed sleeves and a long white ruffled pinafore.

"Kathy, you look very Christmasy," said Sara.

"Michelle gave it to me," said Kathy, then whispered to Sara, "Daddy made me wear it."

"Very pretty," said Sara. "Perfect for Christmas."

"Hot," complained Kathy as she helped to carry in the gifts. "What's in this big one?"

"Why don't you open it and see?" said Michelle, somewhat irritated by Kathy's ingratitude for the dress.

Cocktails were being served on the veranda. Louella had enlisted the aid of her eldest son, a lanky boy with soft eyes and a gentle manner. He served fresh Iranian caviar, a gift from the Martines, and tiny hot biscuits with ham and crabmeat.

"Now? Can we open our presents now?" begged Kathy, dancing eagerly in front of her father.

"Mac isn't here yet."

"No need to wait for Mac," said Michelle. "You know how he is about time."

Chris nodded rather grimly. "All right, Kathy, suppose you begin? I'm sure you know exactly which are yours. Then you can play Santa and deliver our presents. And please ask Louella to join us now."

When everyone was comfortably seated around Kathy's stack of presents, she began opening them with extra squeals of delight for the easel and paints from Sara. Chris had give his daughter a number of expensive toys, but the one she seemed to like best, surprisingly, was a stuffed bear.

"Paddington! Daddy, where did you find him?" With the possessive fervor of a much younger child Kathy hugged the jaunty, traveling bear. "I missed him so much!"

"He's not the same—" Chris began.

"Yes! Yes, he is!" Kathy held the bear out to Toby, who shared her excitement by racing through the discarded wrappings. "Look, Toby, he's really back!"

Sara suspected that somehow Kathy had lost her former toy and Chris had not realized its importance to the lonely little girl—until now.

"Children grow up too fast these days," Mrs. Latham commented more to herself than anyone else.

Kathy had no choice, thought Sara.

Kathy enjoyed distributing presents to the grown-ups. Louella showed her immediate pleasure by wearing Sara's pink scarf and Chris's present of a handmade stole both at the same time. Toby unwrapped his bones with considerably more enthusiasm than Michelle exhibited when she accepted Chris's gift of diamond earrings.

Chris presented his mother with an elegant photo album covered in Japanese silk brocade, which contained his own prize-winning photographic work. Sara envied that gift, but contented herself with leafing through the album, delighted to see the proof of Chris's artistic talent.

Kathy had collected shells, grasses, and small bits of flotsam to make a collage, a souvenir of the island for Sara. Mrs. Latham gave Sara a square of needlepoint with a shell design. She felt very touched by her gifts from the Lathams, a family who could afford anything, but gave of themselves, the most valuable gift of all.

Except for Chris. As though fearing commitment of any kind as far as she was concerned, he gave her a large, expensive bottle of Miss Dior perfume, certainly worthy of appreciation. But Sara could see him having some secretary order dozens of bottles.

Sara's gift to Chris, the presentation note explaining that the portrait of Kathy and Toby would be late, seemed to move him.

"Sara, I can think of no finer gift," he said with apparent sincerity, and rose to gently kiss her cheek. In so doing, he noticed Mac's ring on her right hand.

He straightened abruptly. "Christmas present, Sara?"

"Yes, from Mac."

"It looks like an engagement ring."

"Exactly what it was supposed to be," Michelle explained to Chris. "But Sara needs a little more time. Despite the fact that I have been telling her all morning what a great catch my brother is."

"And where is he now?" asked Chris, sounding irritated.

Michelle appeared amused. "Mac doesn't live by the clock," she said archly, making it sound like a criticism of her host. "But I'm sure he'll be along soon."

"Tell us about your new shop," Mrs. Latham urged Michelle.

Michelle needed no second invitation. "Well, Mother, the style show is on Friday, as you know," Michelle said with the most enthusiasm she had yet displayed. "All the fabrics are from my new Haitian line, even the special wedding dress."

"Will you wear that dress at your wedding?" asked Mrs. Latham.

"No, Mother. Since I've been married before, I won't wear white. Dear me! We must talk. I have been so busy, I almost forgot my own wedding!" She smiled enchantingly at all of them.

Michelle's use of "Mother" turned a knife in Sara's breast. It sounded so false! A terrible shuddery feeling came over Sara, and she wasn't certain that she could survive this day with Michelle and Chris together.

"Father Gregory and I haven't even discussed the wedding," continued Michelle in her light, cultivated voice. "Chris, the darling, handled all the boring details." She looked up at him adoringly. "But I have planned the colors. Of course it is to be a simple island wedding with just a few friends and family."

"And a horde of photographers," added Mrs. Latham.

"Naturally, Mother. In my position," said Michelle, trying ineffectually to look modest, "photographers are to be expected."

Chris said nothing but did not appear particularly happy. Kathy climbed on his lap to show him the many colors in her paint set, which barely held his attention.

"The wedding will be in shades of blue and lavender," said Michelle waving her hands theatrically. "I shall wear a cocktail-length lavender-blue chiffon. In my hair and bouquet will be the rare Cyanea blue orchids. My bridesmaids will wear the blue of a summer sky and carry sprays of Cattleya orchids. Mother, you will wear periwinkle."

Mrs. Latham's back stiffened. "I bought beige," she said flatly. "Goes with anything."

"Don't worry, Mother," Michelle retorted smoothly. "Your periwinkle dress is hanging in your closet. I am certain you'll like it."

Mrs. Latham simmered in frustration but made no reply.

Michelle seemed not to notice. "I wonder where Mac can be," she said distantly.

"When Mac is sailing, he loses track of everything but the joy of it," said Sara. "And the more difficult it is, the better he likes it."

Chris remarked with a thin smile, "Who would know that better than you?"

"Uncle Mac!" cried Kathy, jumping up to race toward the door where Mac stood.

Mac picked her up and held her high. "Merry Christmas, pretty girl." He gave Kathy a kiss.

Sara thought that Mac looked great, not at all "depressed" as Michelle had claimed. His personality sparkled as brightly as his clothes. After making witty responses to the ladies' compliments, he bent to kiss Sara. It was a warm, deep kiss.

Leaving her blushing, Mac said, "And a Merry Christmas to you too, my very pretty girl."

Chris did not join in the light gaiety of the moment. "What are you drinking?" he asked Mac irritably.

"Sorry if I've kept you waiting," Mac apologized.

"Don't let Chris bully you, Mac," said Mrs. Latham. "We have all the time in the world. Roast turkey is probably one of the few animals that improve with age."

"Thanks, Nana." Mac kissed her lightly and mixed himself a drink at the bar. "Stopped by the cay," he said. "Gala preparations for tonight. Lots of new boats in the harbor. And the little pigs are already revolving on their spits."

"Will you dance with me tonight, Uncle Mac?" piped Kathy.

"Don't I always?"

At the dinner table Chris sat at the head with Michelle and his mother on either side. On this occasion Kathy made no effort to say her blessing, having been previously coached, perhaps, by Chris or her grandmother. Chris made some appropriate Christmasy comments before dinner, competently playing his role as host. He carved the huge turkey with ease and grace. He said all the proper things to his guests, was gravely polite and respectful to his mother, thoughtful of his daughter, and carefully attentive to his fiancée.

And yet, thought Sara, he seemed remote, as though he might have been seeing other Christmases, happier times. Michelle appeared bored; Mrs. Latham, tense. Only Mac and Kathy seemed natural, oblivious to the treacherous crosscurrents swirling around them.

The food was excellent, but after the plum pudding had been flamed and after-dinner drinks offered, Sara was happy to slip away, at Kathy's request, to see her Christmas presents.

In her room Kathy complained to Sara, "*She* is going to be my new mother forever and ever."

Sara sat on Kathy's bed. "Michelle's oaky," she said tactfully. "You could do worse."

"Are you going to marry Uncle Mac?"

"I don't know."

"Can I see your engagement ring?"

Sara held out her right hand. "It's not an engagement ring yet."

"It's big!" said Kathy, twisting the ring. "It sparkles a lot."

"Yes."

"When we all go back to New York, will I see you?" Kathy asked anxiously. "Will you still be my friend?"

Sara tried to hug the worries out of the little girl. "You know I will. We shall always be friends."

Michelle stood in the doorway of Kathy's bedroom. Her expression was disapproving. "Sara, we're leaving now."

* * *

Michelle had been right about Mac's appreciation of Sara's Christmas gift. From his reaction the simple nautical clock might have been gold set with diamonds. And Mac seemed quite content that Sara was wearing his diamond on her right hand instead of her left. That she was wearing it at all seemed enough to satisfy him.

On the veranda Mac, holding his customary frosted glass of rum, asked Sara what she thought of the Latham party. Sara's comment was tactful, but Mac was not fooled.

"What is it you women have about strong, silent, grumpy men?" Mac demanded. "Sure, Chris is rich, good at his work, fairly handsome." He rattled the ice in his drink. "Doesn't drink too much like some of us. Is good to his mother and kid." Mac grinned roguishly. "Honestly, Sara, what makes a cool woman like Michelle go batty over a guy as cold as Chris Latham?"

Sara knew for certain that Chris Latham was far from cold. But she didn't know how to tell Mac. "Has anyone learned the actual date of the wedding?"

"No formal invitations." Mac shrugged. "Just a simple island wedding." He parodied Michelle's words. "With photographers having a field day and the wedding pictures in all the slick magazines."

"Chris must want that too or he wouldn't be marrying Michelle," said Sara sensibly.

"Chris doesn't know what he wants," said Mac, leaning toward Sara and brushing her cheek with his lips. "Marry me, Sara. Wear the ring on your left hand. I know what I want, and you will never be sorry."

How easy it would be to say yes to Mac. It would

solve so many problems. She would have her own life. Mac was lovable and kind. He would not be too difficult to live with. Their life would be easy, uncomplicated, smoothed by the assurance of wealth. Just one complication: She loved Chris Latham, not Mac. She loved that impossible, moody, strange Chris Latham! Mac was right. Women and their loves made no sense.

The Marina Cay cocktail party was in full swing, a noisy, friendly crowd including many children. Clothing ranged from informal beach attire to elegant gowns. Sara was introduced to so many people so fast that they seemed a blur.

Music was continuous, calypso sounds that Sara loved. There were guitars, drums, even a boom-bass, that strange washtub instrument with strings. As a favor to Sara, Mac set down his drink and they danced. Mac appeared to know all of the musicians, or perhaps they recognized a fan, because it was obvious that this music had meaning for Mac. He led Sara in the rhythm, gracefully and expertly, with a light touch that she found exhilarating.

When Chris cut in, Sara, rather surprised to see him, half wished that he would leave them alone. Somehow dancing with Mac seemed safer. But Mac graciously acceded, and Sara waited until Chris took her in his arms.

Chris did not dance as naturally as Mac, but he had a sure touch and his steps were confident. As he looked down into Sara's face he seemed much more interested in what he saw there than the steps they were taking. Sara felt quivery in his arms, light and

140

slightly dizzy, as though without his arms she would fall, motionless.

Feeling slightly guilty, Sara asked, "Where is Michelle?"

"She's around somewhere."

"Is your mother here, and Kathy?" asked Sara politely. "I haven't seen them."

"They're here."

Continuing to dance in silence, Chris held her an inch closer, and Sara missed a step. "Sorry," she murmured.

He didn't reply. Then when they had reached the far end of the patio, which had become crowded with dancers, Chris said impatiently, "I want to talk to you." He took her hand, leading her among cacti and oleander in the garden to an almost hidden bench. "Sit down," he said rather roughly.

Sara did as he ordered, in her haste catching her heel on a rough stone on the patio. "My heel is caught," she said inanely.

Chris stooped to free her shoe. Finding the task difficult in the dim light, his fingers touched her ankle as he slipped off her shoe.

At his touch Sara felt as though a bolt of lightning had shot through her. She gasped. No man had ever caused such a reaction by his slightest touch.

"Don't be afraid," Chris said, misunderstanding. "It's dark here, but we're quite safe. I'll have your heel free in a second."

Of course he had no idea why she had gasped, nor of the seething tortures his touch had produced. Sara was afraid all right, terribly frightened of the uncontrollable reaction he had caused. She must never let him guess.

Slipping her shoe back on easily, Chris again lightly brushed her ankle, causing a sensation that was torture but also ecstasy.

"There," said Chris, sitting beside her on the bench.

"Thank you," murmured Sara.

Chris said seriously, "Sara, I want to talk to you, away from Mac—about Mac—because it's important."

Sara looked at him dutifully, listening but not really hearing. In the moonlight she could see the marvelous planes of his face; the long, high cheekbones; his broad brow; the mass of dark, silky, wavy hair. Seeing him, being so close, quite took her breath away.

". . . must not," he finished and waited for a reply.

Sara simply had not heard, and she couldn't ask him to repeat his words, for he was obviously quite serious and he had expected her to listen. So she waited, hoping he would continue.

"Sara," said Chris, covering her hand with his. "Did you hear what I said?"

There was no escape. Sara replied, "I'm sorry, I don't know what you mean."

"Sara, please don't misinterpret my words," said Chris slowly. "Mac is a good man, intelligent, even talented. But he has serious problems." Chris paused for a moment, gazing down at Sara, then continued. "It is none of my business, I know, and it hurts me to say these things to you. But I have thought about it a lot, and I know beyond the question of a doubt that you must not marry Mac Martine."

"Isn't that my decision?" said Sara. *What right does*

he have to criticize Mac? Loyalty was one of Sara's strongest traits, and it flared now in full force.

"Of course it's your decision," said Chris reasonably. "But I know the situation better than you think."

"You don't know anything," snapped Sara, then felt cold horror when she heard her own cutting words.

Chris withdrew his hand from hers. "Sara, I was only trying to protect you. I—I feel a sort of responsibility for you," he finished painfully.

"You needn't bother," said Sara with a cold cruelty she had never known before. "You have enough problems of your own." She was thinking of Michelle, and it made her furious.

"Sara," begged Chris uncertainly.

Sara knew that she had hurt him. But he had no right! "Worry about your own marriage!" she lashed out with unaccustomed ruthlessness.

A rustling of some tall shrubs was followed by the appearance of Mac. "So, there you are!" he exclaimed heartily.

Sara and Chris looked at him as though he were a stranger.

"Practically scoured all of Diddledoe," said Mac amiably, "until I remembered this secluded nook. Chris, damned if you're not a sly old dog!"

Chris stood to quietly confront Mac's ebullience. He said nothing.

"What you doing here with my fiancée, old buddy?" asked Mac, but he did not smile. Sara couldn't gauge the exact extent of Mac's apparent good humor.

"Sara is not your fiancée yet," said Chris.

"A mere technicality, old boy," Mac replied. "Incidentally your mother and Kathy are ready to leave now."

Chris said nothing, and Sara saw his fists clench at his sides. Then he relaxed, politely thanked Mac, and said equably, "Then I'll take them back. Good night, Sara."

Sara stared after him with a dreadful sense of loss, but Mac grasped her hand and they sat together on the bench.

"Like it here, Sara?"

"What do you mean?"

"This island. Tortolans used to call it Diddledoe, nothing but sand, a few moran trees, and scrub. Then a young couple bought all six acres for sixty dollars and built themselves a dream home right here. The hotel was built around it." Mac's arm encircled Sara's shoulders. "You and I should have such a honeymoon."

"Mac, please don't rush me," Sara implored.

"Would I do that to you?" Mac inquired tenderly. He kissed her lips, lightly possessive.

For Sara the night and Christmas had ended.

CHAPTER NINE

Mac knocked on Sara's door as he opened it. "Mornin'," he said pleasantly. "Kathy wants you to come out and play."

Sara blinked her eyes and replied grumpily, "Tell her to go play with her father and Michelle."

"Can't," said Mac, leaning lazily against the door. "They're playing on Tortola today. I thought we might go sailing—without Kathy, of course."

"Tell her I'm coming out," said Sara, yawning.

They had been up half the night, dancing. Michelle had discovered Raoul, the South American yacht owner who looked like a movie star. They made a striking couple and danced with expert charm and grace far into the night. Lights had flickered off all over the cay before Mac left with Sara, and still Michelle lingered with her newfound friend. Chris had not returned to the cay after seeing his mother and child home.

On this morning after Christmas, Sara dressed quickly in a T-shirt and jeans, brushed her hair, and added a little lipstick. She looked a lot fresher than she felt.

Kathy and Mac sat at the breakfast table on the veranda, eating toast and marmalade.

"No muffins today?"

"Holiday for the Tortolans," Mac explained. "Everybody's off today."

"Could we paint, Sara?" asked Kathy eagerly. "I want to try out my new Christmas paints."

Sara nodded. "And I want to work on your portrait. Do you think you can stay still?"

"Sure," Kathy promised. "It's not so hard being a model."

This statement brought Sara's thoughts back to Michelle and made her wonder what she and Chris were doing on Tortola. *Forget him!* she ordered herself.

"Come along with us, Mac," Sara suggested.

"No," Mac replied haughtily. "If you will not sail with me, I shall spend the day sulking."

"I'll sail with you, Uncle Mac," Kathy said swiftly.

"You will not," Mac replied. "You know that your father won't let you go sailing."

"He's an old fraidy-cat," declared Kathy disloyally.

"Sure," agreed Mac, shrugging. "But what can you do? Go along, Sara. I know you want to finish the portrait. See you later."

At the Latham house Nana was relaxing with a book. "Morning, Sara. They tell me this is another holiday on these islands. For me, it's a day of rest too. Sit down, dear."

"Good morning, Mrs. Latham. Such a lovely, quiet day. It is nice after all the rush."

"Tomorrow it all begins again," said Chris's mother. "You are going to the style show, I suppose." Sara nod-

146

ded. Mrs. Latham continued, "Then there's the opening of Michelle's shop, and the New Year's Eve ball, and the wedding after that. That girl is an organizational wonder. Don't know how she does it. Why, she's even organized that crazy son of mine, who hates being organized by anyone but himself."

Sara thought that his mother's version of Chris was one that she would never have recognized. To her, Chris appeared extremely orderly, almost stuffy, compared to Mac's freewheeling ways.

"When is the wedding?" Sara asked.

"January third."

"And what color are you wearing?" Sara asked with a twinkle in her eye.

Mrs. Latham laughed. "Need you ask? That girl convinced me that I'll look gorgeous in periwinkle."

"You will," said Sara. "It should be nice with your hair."

"At any rate I would never dare to disturb the color scheme for the wedding," said Mrs. Latham. "It is easy to see why that girl is so successful."

Sara could see it too.

The day passed peacefully. With Kathy's now experienced modeling, and the promise of a painting lesson if they finished in time, Sara was able to bring the portrait to a point where she could finish it without further modeling. Sara then asked Mrs. Latham if she would mind posing, and Nana thought it might be fun.

"Get out your things, Kathy," Sara suggested, "and we'll both paint her."

Chris's mother had a lovely composed face with few wrinkles, considering her age. Her eyes were large, a somewhat lighter blue than Chris's startling irises. Sara asked her to sit in one of the white wicker chairs on the veranda, hoping to give the portrait a delicate Victorian quality. Behind her was the papaya tree with a few yellow blossoms, and beyond that, in the turquoise Marina Cay harbor, was the South American's yacht, which looked like a shimmering white toy in the distance.

The style show on Tortola the next day was a gala event, but not entirely planned and modeled by Michelle, as Sara had been led to believe. It was held in a large restaurant built around an old fort near the water. Hundreds of people attended. Some sat in folding chairs, some milled around. Four groups of musicians took turns playing their specialties from rock to classical music, with calypso setting the tone. A large stage had been built, on which the models paraded in front of a rough-hewn stone wall. Most of the clothing had an exotic flavor, not only Michelle's Haitian fabrics, but also African and South Sea island designs.

Opening the show was a proud, stately British gentleman with white muttonchop sideburns. Sara missed some of the long introduction, but obviously he was an important politician. His wife stood beside him, the perfect political mate in her well-bred clothing. She sat demurely, having adjusted her skirt and folded her gloved fingers, while he spoke at length on how hard everyone had worked to produce this successful show.

Photographers flitted around the stage, some obviously local, others more sophisticated. Of the thirty models, Michelle received the greatest applause. Certainly she was the most professional. Obviously Michelle Martine was recognized even in these little-known islands. Michelle wore to perfection her glamorous bare-midriff designs made of Haitian fabrics. They were all there, applauding: Chris, Nana, Kathy, Mac, even the dashing South American, who applauded loudest of all.

The style show ended with her modeling the wedding gown of exquisite fine white cotton with bands of delicate handmade lace, a pristine long veil with silk orange blossoms, and a bouquet of white orchids. At first there was a hush of awed silence, then a murmur swept through the crowd, and at last a great burst of applause.

Sara loved the gown. But somehow Michelle did not look quite right in it. That wedding gown required more innocence than Michelle could ever manage. Clever of her to wear the sophisticated lavender chiffon at her own wedding.

The narrator of the style show, a neat, stylish blue-haired woman, made a little speech saying that the show had ended, and she again thanked all of the shops, hairdressers, and local people who had made the show such a great success.

"And a special thank you to Ms. Michelle Martine the well-known international model, who so graciously modeled her own Haitian designs today. All of these creations will be available at the new shop Ms. Martine is opening this evening right here in Road Town." She paused as someone backstage spoke to her. "Another announcement: If any of you are interested in purchasing the wedding gown you just saw, I am sorry, but it has already been purchased. I am told that you may order a copy, but it will take some time, because it is completely handmade in Haiti."

The audience applauded again, then a murmur swept through the crowd and a buzz of remarks were directed toward the stage. "You want to know the purchaser of the wedding gown?" the narrator asked, sounding folksy and smiling broadly at the applause. "I don't know if I should divulge that at this time," she said coyly. Then evidently she had some sort of signal because she continued, "I am happy to tell you that the purchaser is an old friend of our islands, a man who has been coming here for many years. Mister MacKinley Martine has purchased the gown for his bride-to-be, Miss Sara Ann Williston."

A great roar of applause went up. Sara felt as though she had been struck by a truck. Did she cry out? She didn't know. But she felt the swift flush in her face, and then she turned in stunned wonder to Mac, who sat beside her, smiling expansively. As the applause continued he took her hand and they stood together. Sara was too amazed to speak.

Mac appeared quite pleased with himself. "I knew it was the perfect wedding gown for you," he whispered to Sara. "I couldn't let it get away."

Slowly Sara recovered from the shock. She wanted to scream her outrage at Mac, but he looked so happy and he had made this public announcement with all the best intentions. In the end she simply shook her head at him and asked quietly, "What if we don't get married?"

But Mac was already accepting congratulations from a number of people. Sara wondered if this was how most people married: Because it was time? Because others expected it of them? Because someone couldn't say no? Because it was easier than any other alternative? Marrying Mac now seemed like the simplest thing to do.

Through the crush of people wishing them well, Sara saw Chris's face as he moved toward them. He looked dark and disapproving, and Sara would have avoided him if she could.

Chris suggested caustically, "Maybe you should move your engagement ring to the proper finger."

"Chris, I had no idea—"

"Michelle is a marvelous saleswoman," he said evenly. "Undoubtedly I will see you and Mac tonight when she opens her shop." He gave Sara a sardonic smile. "Champagne, I understand, will flow like water. A proper toast to our mutual weddings."

Mrs. Latham kissed Sara lightly. "May you have much happiness, dear Sara," she said with a quick smile. Then to Chris, "Let's get out of this mob scene."

Kathy looked up to Sara with a puzzled expression. She said as though betrayed, "Everybody's getting married."

Sara was left with Mac, who seemed to be shaking hands with everyone in Tortola.

At Michelle's shop the crowd was fantastic. Champagne flowed generously, as Chris had predicted. Michelle, happy and successful, played the owner-hostess role flawlessly.

As the evening wore on and the Lathams did not appear Sara wondered if Chris had taken his mother and Kathy back to Great Camanoe. She thought it odd that he would not be by his fiancée's side in her time of triumph. The South American, Raoul Perez, stood beside Michelle, giving her his undivided attention.

Since Michelle had no immediate need for Sara, she found Mac and asked if they could leave. He acceded to her wishes instantly. They found a taxi, which took them to a hotel overlooking the water. Here they had dinner in a quiet dining room with gracious service. During dessert Sara asked Mac about the wedding gown.

"It was rather gauche of me," he readily admitted. "At least the way it came out in public. I am sorry about that."

"But, Mac, you know that we aren't even engaged," Sara pointed out. "You promised to leave it up to me."

Mac looked like a small boy about to be spanked. "The wedding dress had to be yours," he said defensively. "It was so perfect for you that I had to buy it before someone else did."

That was the exact reason he had given for asking her to be engaged. Mac seemed to want to secure things, and people, to tie them up quickly so that no one else could take them from him. Sara recognized possessiveness and insecurity in this man who showed the world a seemingly careless self-confidence. His drinking probably stemmed from the same insecurity. Far from being turned off by her discovery about Mac, Sara felt a new understanding and a desire to help him.

"You shouldn't have bought the dress," Sara said kindly, "but I think I understand why you did. You are a generous person. But it must have been terribly expensive, and I really don't feel right about accepting the dress, nor this ring." She nervously touched the large diamond.

Mac looked hurt. "Sara, darling, these material things mean nothing. Don't you know that?"

Sara nodded, serious, but smiling to herself. "Mac, please don't be clever with me."

"Okay," he agreed with a grin. "You know that I will do everything in my power to make you my wife. But don't forget," he said softly, "I love you very much." He reached across the table, took her right hand in his, and, slowly, with his loving eyes never leaving hers, he removed the ring and placed it on her left hand. "Wear the ring, Sara. Be my wife."

Sara gazed into Mac's hazel eyes, soft with tenderness. It had been a day of strong persuasion, and she was weary. She did not remove the ring.

CHAPTER TEN

Michelle, preoccupied with her wedding, gave Sara small sketching assignments, which she quickly completed. Sara would have welcomed more work to occupy her troubled mind. In the lull she finished Kathy's portrait almost to her satisfaction. She never felt completely satisfied with any of her work, but there had to be a stopping point. Sometimes when she tried too long to perfect a portrait, she lost the essential ingredient. So she put aside Kathy's portrait, waiting for the proper time to present it to Chris.

Chris and Michelle were evidently off on projects of their own. Although Sara worked many hours at the Latham house on Nana's portrait, Chris was always elsewhere. Sara enjoyed the older woman, who was honest, outspoken, and unexpectedly humorous. Kathy added her own brand of childish glee to their gatherings, and Sara was almost happy. The South American, Raoul Perez, lingered on. His luxurious yacht, moored in the Marina Cay harbor, was a constant reminder of his presence.

The approaching New Year's Eve ball, a charity event, had great social significance and a rather snobbish colonial protocol, which amused both Sara and Michelle. Nevertheless Michelle was very careful to adhere to all of the island's strict social rules. Many pre-ball parties required responses, and Sara took on the temporary duties of a social secretary.

Sitting on the bed in Michelle's room, Sara tried to assure her hostess that it wasn't really necessary for her to attend the ball. But Michelle would have none of that. Leafing through the many long dresses in her closet, Michelle brought forth a plastic bag, whipped off the covering, and exclaimed, *"Voilà!"*

A gossamer shell-pink chiffon, which Michelle waved enticingly in front of Sara, glimmered with soft silver lights. The gown was simple but ravishing.

"That is the most beautiful dress I have ever seen in my life," said Sara in a small voice hushed with awe.

"Isn't it!" agreed Michelle. "Almost forgot I had it. A Paris memory, worn once. Try it on."

"Michelle, I couldn't! It's too elegant, too sophisticated for me." Sara laughed self-consciously. "I wouldn't know how to behave in a dress like that."

"All the better reason to wear it," said Michelle crisply. "Now off with your clothes. Let's see how it fits."

At Michelle's insistence, and with her determined help, Sara tried on the dress. Michelle gave her a pair of high-heeled sandals, swept Sara's hair back, and clipped on a pair of dangling diamond earrings.

Sara looked into the mirror and found herself suddenly transformed.

"Come on," said Michelle. "Let's show Mac."

Sara, wobbling uncertainly in the shoes, which didn't exactly fit, followed Michelle to the veranda.

Michelle said, "Cinderella goes to the ball."

Mac gazed at Sara silently for a moment, then said, "Good Lord! You can't wear that to the ball. Every man in the islands will fall at your feet!"

Sara laughed. "It's not exactly me."

"It *is* you," said Mac, suddenly serious. "It is the new glamorous you who will be my wife. Oh, Sara," he said huskily and took her into his arms, kissing her with new passion under Michelle's knowing eye. "Marry me," he urged ardently. "Right away. Today!"

"Mac, do be serious," said Sara, pushing away.

"Tomorrow, then," he insisted. "I am serious."

Sara thought that perhaps he was. Michelle had left them. Sara felt very alone with Mac. And afraid, not of him, but of her lack of emotion—her lack of the love that he so needed and was demanding.

"Please, Mac," she begged as tears clouded her vision. She turned and ran to her bedroom. Mac did not follow. After she carefully removed Michelle's dress, fearful that tears would stain the precious fabric, she lay on the bed and abandoned herself to sobs of frustration.

Michelle, standing in the half light from louvered shutters, looked rather old and tired. "You don't love him at all, do you?" she asked quietly.

Sara nodded. "I do, but not like he wants me to."

"He knows that," said Michelle sensibly. "He can wait. He only wants to marry you first."

Sara felt her face crumple again. "I can't," she replied tearfully. "It isn't honest. I just can't."

"He can be very lovable," said Michelle. "He can be everything you want in a man. He needs you."

"I know all that," Sara said almost angrily. "But I can't do it. I don't know what I will do. But I can't marry Mac."

"It's Chris, isn't it?" asked Michelle, but she already knew the answer. Sara's face only confirmed it. "I knew it," said Michelle. "And I understand how you feel. You must hate me."

"No."

"Chris Latham is a very disturbing man." Michelle gazed sternly at Sara. "There is nothing you can do, you know. Chris and I will be married in very few days."

"I know," Sara murmured. "I think I should leave. I'll go home."

Michelle's eyebrows lifted. "Aren't Gwen and your father still on their honeymoon?"

Sara had forgotten. She didn't even know where they were. She said miserably, "I have a key."

"You can't go home to an empty house. Not in your

present state anyway. Stay here, and I will make Mac let you alone—no more trying to push you into a marriage that you're not ready for."

"Poor Mac," said Sara. "I wish I could." And she added honestly, "It's too difficult to see you and Chris together. I must go."

"Do what you must," said Michelle with icy menace. "But just remember: There is *nothing* you can do about Chris and me."

That afternoon Chris stopped by. Sara thought he looked marvelous, tanned and healthy. The almost perpetual lines of fatigue had eased, and his wonderful smile lit up the room. She would never get over him.

Chris told Sara he had a surprise for her. Following him to the patio, Sara saw two people standing beside Captain Hook's perch.

"Daddy!" Sara rushed to embrace her father.

After he had thoroughly hugged and kissed his daughter, Mr. Williston explained that their houseboat was anchored just below, near the jetty, and this nice young man had kindly given them a lift to the Martine house.

"Hello, Gwen," said Sara, thinking that her young stepmother seemed not so ominous anymore. Perhaps it was because her father looked so happy.

Michelle and Mac joined them, suggesting that everyone come inside for some refreshment. Chris could not stay, and Michelle walked with him to his car. Sara turned to her father and Gwen.

The Willistons had chartered a houseboat in St. Thomas and, like many honeymooners, found the quiet, almost forgotten islands of the B.V.I. a perfect paradise. While Gwen and her old friends, the Martines, reminisced, Sara had an opportunity to ask her father if he was really happy.

"Very," he said. "And I've taken up tennis—not as good as Gwen yet, but I'm learning fast."

"You look wonderful, Daddy," said Sara, pleased that her father had found Gwen and that they were so compatible. Sara thought that perhaps she might have grown up a lot in these past few days, loving Chris and knowing he could never be hers. Her former childish jealousy of Gwen seemed to have disappeared.

Her father, always the art professor, asked about her painting. Sara took him to her room. Grateful for the moment alone with her father, she showed him both Kathy's and Nana's portraits.

"Excellent use of light, the hard white of the balustrade, sunlight on the leaves, tone and texture of the woman's dress." Her father nodded appreciatively.

Sara thanked him. But then he thought Kathy's portrait might have been overworked. "Something in the eyes," he said critically.

"Eyes are the hardest. She's not as happy as a child should be."

Her father did not inquire further, but touched Sara's hand encouragingly. "You are a good artist, Sara, and if you keep at it, you might even be a great one."

"Parental pride," said Sara modestly, "but I intend to keep painting, no matter what."

"Good girl." Her father lifted her hand. "Now tell me truthfully, young lady, what is the meaning of this gigantic diamond?"

Sara had forgotten the ring. Although she had her

doubts about marrying Mac, she continued to wear his ring. Now she tried to explain to her father. But she did not mention Chris because he could have no part in her decision.

Her father, looking wise and handsome, and somehow younger than ever, said, "Mac is older of course. But, as we know, that is not such a bad thing in a husband."

"Age has nothing to do with it, Daddy."

"And with you, love has everything to do with it." Her father smiled and patted her hand reassuringly. "I know, darling. If you must wait for love, then you must wait. Don't rush into anything. And don't feel that you should leave home because of Gwen. There will always be a loving place for you in our home."

Sara nodded. "I know that, Daddy. But I think I would like to get off on my own, if I can find the right place."

"Take your time and think about it," her father urged. "You have a good head on your shoulders. You will do the right thing."

"Thanks, Daddy." She knew he meant well, and he was always unfailingly supportive. But it wasn't her head that was causing all the trouble.

Michelle asked everyone to stay for dinner and also invited the Lathams. But Chris came alone, saying that Kathy had a cold, and she and Nana had eaten earlier. John Paul, faced with three unexpected guests, added a few shrimp to the two large lobsters he had expected to serve for dinner and delighted everyone with lobster cardinale.

"Congratulations on your forthcoming wedding,"

said Mr. Williston to Chris. "Certainly your bride-to-be is one of the most beautiful women in the world."

Michelle thanked him sweetly. "If you'll be around on January third, you are invited to the wedding."

"Let's stay, Robert," urged Gwen. "How could we miss the celebrity wedding of the year?"

Chris gave them his polite smile. A smile of forbearance, thought Sara. Gwen sounded like a teen-age groupie. But Michelle seemed pleased.

"Well," said Mr. Williston, "if we're staying, why don't all of you join us tomorrow? We're planning to visit Norman Island. Our captain tells us some tall stories about pirate treasure and caves over there."

"Tomorrow night is New Year's Eve," said Michelle. "There's a big charity ball on Tortola. Won't you join us?"

Gwen said excitedly, "Why can't we do both?"

"You must excuse me," said Mac. "I have some business in Saint Thomas tomorrow. But I'll be back in time for the ball."

Chris said thoughtfully, "Perhaps I could make it."

"Then do!" urged Michelle. "I have an appointment with the hairdresser."

"Then, it's settled," said Mr. Williston. "We'll leave around eight if that's all right with everyone."

The Willistons showed Chris and Sara around their houseboat, a luxurious 34-foot Chris-Craft, which boasted wall-to-wall carpet and all amenities, including stereo-tape music and air conditioning. They were introduced to the young captain and his wife, whose culinary reputation was extolled by both Willistons.

Cruising southwest through the Sir Francis Drake Channel was a pleasant, stately experience, quite different from Mac's almost death-defying sailboat skirmishes. The weather was clear and hot, and the constant tradewinds were a blessing. They anchored at Treasure Point on Norman Island's north shore, close to the caves and adjacent to good diving spots.

The Willistons, Chris, and Sara took the dinghy to explore the caves. In the smaller boat the water seemed unusually rough. While Chris rowed, he related the colorful story of Norman, the buccaneer, who had buried his treasure on the island around 1843.

Bats inhabited the caves, and Gwen soon found that she wasn't as eager to explore all of the caves as she had at first believed. In fact, she said, she felt a little seasick. The Willistons decided to return to the houseboat to rest. Chris and Sara took the dinghy out again to dive in a special cove that Chris liked.

The cove, ringed with coconut palms, looked like something out of the South Seas. Pelicans eyed them comically, and a large white ibis stalked disdainfully down the beach, oblivious of the human invaders. When they dived, scattering small parrot fish, the underwater landscape revealed what looked like miles of elkhorn coral. French angels, snappers, and the four-eyed butterfly fish welcomed the newcomers in their world.

Back on the beach, resting under a palm tree, Sara said, "How lucky you are to live here."

"After this year I don't think I will be living here anymore."

Sara thought first of Kathy and how she loved Great Camanoe, despite the lack of friends her own age. "How can you give up all this?"

"Want to buy my house?" asked Chris jokingly.

If only she could! And keep him in it of course. "A little too rich for my blood. But won't Kathy miss being here?"

"Kathy is a lot like her mother," said Chris. "Now that she's growing up she's too adventuresome. When I'm away on business, I worry about her."

Sara could understand that. "But you will have Michelle."

"Michelle wants only to visit. Too isolated."

Sara felt sorry for Kathy.

"Sara, I wish you liked me better," Chris said unexpectedly. "You think I'm strange, cold, maybe even cruel. Don't deny it! I have seen you with Kathy, and I feel your disapproval of me as a father." His electric blue eyes raked her face. "And from that stern expression I know what you're thinking now."

Did he really! How surprised he would be to know *all* of her thoughts at this moment! Sara was trapped: She could not possibly reveal her serious doubts about Michelle as a stepmother nor her own longings for him. But she could tell him how she felt about Kathy. In fact she must, because this might be her last chance. And for Kathy's sake, some things needed to be said.

"Chris, I don't think that you know my thoughts," said Sara gently. "But there is something about Kathy, something that I think I may understand because my mother died when I was very young. And my father loved me dearly, as you do Kathy."

"You are still very young," said Chris.

"You can't keep Kathy protected forever," said Sara earnestly. "You can't put her in a safe place, no matter how pleasant and comfortable, and keep her there until you are ready to take her out again. As you said, Kathy is curious and very intelligent. She needs adventure to live and grow. We all do."

"Adventure?" said Chris thoughtfully. "There are many kinds of adventure, mental and physical. The only adventure I withhold from Kathy is sailing, and I have a very good reason for that."

"*Your* reason—or hers?"

"Mine," said Chris tersely.

"Kathy has begged both Mac and me to take her sailing."

"But she didn't go," said Chris confidently.

"One day she will."

"How can you know that?" Chris demanded angrily. An expression of pain crossed his face. "Kathy obeys me."

"Is that what you want? Blind obedience?"

Chris turned to her impatiently. "Dammit, Sara! What are you trying to say?"

Sara backed away imperceptibly from his anger. "Perhaps I had no right," she said tentatively.

Chris leaned back against the palm tree with an exasperated sigh. "I want to tell you so that you'll understand." He hesitated for a long moment. "Kathy's mother drowned in a sailing accident. No matter how irrational I may seem to you, I cannot let my daughter ever enter a sailboat."

So that was it! "I'm sorry," said Sara softly. "Does Kathy know how her mother died?"

"Kathy was a baby. Later I told her there was a

boating accident, but we never spoke of it again. And Kathy never asked again."

Knowing Kathy, Sara felt that although the little girl had not asked, she would have extracted, somehow, all the details about her mother's death. And despite her father's restrictions, even with the knowledge of her mother's drowning in a sailboat, Sara had no doubt that one day Kathy Latham would sail a boat.

"Unfortunately," Chris continued, "Kathy loves the water as her mother before her. But with Michelle's help, and by selling our house here, I think we can steer Kathy's interests into safer channels—on land."

Impossible! thought Sara. Water was Kathy's element. "Fear is the worst thing that could happen to Kathy," Sara declared. "You can't want your daughter to grow up with your fears! Teach her the rudiments of safe sailing. Suffer your own fears if you must, but don't cripple your daughter with them."

Chris's face seemed to whiten under his tan. "You *are* very young," he said tautly, "and also very cruel. You know nothing of tragedy and sorrow."

"Forgive me," said Sara contritely. "The last thing I wanted to do was hurt you." She looked up to him, hoping for some understanding, but there was none. She said quietly, "Perhaps we should go back now."

Without a word Chris picked up their gear, and he rowed in silence back to the houseboat. The Willistons were having lunch on deck.

"Sorry we couldn't wait," said Gwen, who evidently had completely recovered. "This conch chowder is delicious. Do try some. And the lobster salad is wonderful."

Chris said grimly that he wasn't hungry and asked

164

to be excused. He went below without a further word to any of them.

Sara forced herself to have lunch with her father and Gwen, making polite conversation and excuses for Chris. Probably she had been wrong to speak her thoughts about fears so frankly. But Kathy was such a healthy little girl so far, despite her father's overprotectiveness. And she didn't want Kathy to change.

They returned to the Camanoe jetty with plenty of time to get ready for the cocktail party on Tortola. Chris bade them all a restrained good-bye. Sara made arrangements for the Martines to pick up the Willistons in Mac's powerboat because the houseboat captain would not cruise at night.

When Sara returned to the Martine house, Michelle had already left for the cocktail party. Sara realized that she would need to hurry. Sun and sea had taken their usual toll, and she hoped she would not be too sunburned for the elegant pink and silver gown that lay on her bed.

Mac waved a shoe box. "Hey there, Cinderella, come try on your slippers."

"Too sandy," Sara protested. "Wait until I shower."

"Now," Mac ordered. Nudging Sara into a chair, he pulled a towel from her beach bag and, kneeling, began to wipe the sand from her feet.

"Mac," Sara objected, for he was already dressed for the party, "let me do that."

"You have lovely feet," said Mac, continuing as though he hadn't heard. "Now, let's see if this strap of silver fits."

Sara looked down on Mac's shining blond hair and

wondered again why she couldn't simply marry him and settle things.

The sandals fit perfectly. Sara said guardedly, "They look terribly extravagant."

"They were," said Mac happily.

"I'll give you a check for them," said Sara, afraid to ask how much.

"You will not! They are a Christmas gift." He reached into his pocket. "Picked up another trinket." Mac opened the velvet jewel box when Sara did not move.

A pair of diamond drop earrings glittered against black velvet.

"Mac, this is too much! I can't possibly accept these gifts." Mac looked boyishly disappointed, incongruous without his party smile. Sara sighed with tolerant exasperation. "Mac, are you trying to buy me?"

"Whatever the price, I'll gladly pay it," he replied with a quick grin.

Sara told him seriously, "Mac, I am not wearing your ring tonight, nor these lovely earrings. You promised me time to decide, and you're rushing me."

"Bribing and rushing," he agreed cheerfully. "Wear the earrings, Sara. Michelle's dress demands nothing less."

CHAPTER ELEVEN

Underneath Mac's casual exterior was a stubborn determination that Sara recognized, but nevertheless acceded to—in part. She would wear the earrings in honor of the dress. But not the engagement ring, because she would not be pushed that far. And Mac appeared mollified, at least for the present.

Sara's beach-ruined hair needed work. But with the help of Michelle's blow-dryer and the soft cistern water that poured off the roofs of island houses, her hair soon gleamed. Michelle's pink and silver gown fit so perfectly and floated so gracefully when she moved that Sara felt as though she were flying.

Mac was not entirely satisfied. "Permit me," he said, and swept her long hair back and up, securing it with a diamond clip from Michelle's jewelry box.

In the mirror Sara saw a more mature, sophisticated woman. What was it? The hairdo? The diamond drop earrings? The designer gown? No, there was something about the expression too. Sara was amazed—and a little unsure of this strange new person.

"Mac, do I really look all right? Not too severe?"

"Breathtaking is the word," declared Mac. "Tonight, my love, I think you will find that you, not Michelle, are the belle of the ball."

All Sara could think of at the moment was that Michelle was still Chris Latham's belle, and that was all that mattered. Surely no mere dress and hairdo could change that fact.

How strange it was to be so dressed up and have to negotiate boats and jetties and taxis to get to a party. Island living was not always simple. The Willistons, Mac, and Sara arrived quite late at the administrator's cocktail party. But a large crowd still milled on the sweeping lawns that surrounded the magnificent mansion house. Like a sugar-white Greek temple with Doric columns, the house stood high on a hill on Tortola's south shore.

Sara looked around for Chris and Michelle but did not see them. Mac introduced her to scores of people, Britons, Tortolans, and Americans. Also a Belgian and a Frenchman. The latter two kissed Sara's hand—her first encounter with this European courtesy.

When they arrived at the ball, Chris was still absent. Michelle, monopolized by the wealthy South American Raoul Perez, seemed not to mind. As Sara danced with Mac, Raoul cut in. He was an excellent dancer, especially good at the calypso beat, and she followed him easily. But his constant, overdone compliments were a little disturbing. Raoul seemed content with nothing less than enchanting every female at the party.

At last Chris arrived and asked Sara to dance. Apparently he had forgiven her for her "cruel" remarks that afternoon. But he seemed distant and preoccupied. With her face close to Chris's ruffled shirtfront, Sara felt almost dizzy from his disturbing male presence. The sure strength of his arms and the litheness of his body as he led her in the dance elated her beyond belief. Content not to talk, she was happy being led wherever he chose. Other dancers whirled by in a blur. Therefore she was somewhat surprised to find herself outside in the garden.

"We must talk," Chris said urgently. He led her along a path to an iron bench that was almost totally enclosed by hibiscus. He had taken her hand and now looked down at her fingers. "Why aren't you wearing your engagement ring?"

"Mac promised me time to decide."

Chris touched an earring. "And these?" he asked, sounding quietly dangerous.

"A gift. He bought them in Saint Thomas today. But I can't keep them."

"Why not? He can afford it."

"It doesn't matter. I can't accept gifts from him if I'm not going to marry him."

"*Are* you going to marry him?" Chris demanded.

"I can't—not yet," said Sara painfully.

"Oh? Somebody at home?" Chris's compelling eyes would not let her look away, although he no longer touched her hand.

"No, no one."

Sara felt his tension relax somewhat, but he still stared at her as though demanding answers.

"You must not marry Mac Martine," said Chris with quiet certainty. "I don't doubt that he loves you.

The way you look tonight—" He paused, frowning, gazing at her as though she presented an insoluble problem. "No matter how much you love Mac," he continued purposefully, "I don't think you are equipped to handle him. He's my friend, and I like him. But I have also known him for many years." Chris heaved an exasperated sigh and slapped his knees in frustration. "You must think I'm crazy."

Sara wondered about his motives. But crazy, no. "What would you have me do?" she asked with interest.

Chris was still staring at her darkly, pondering that question, when they heard the bells toll the new year.

Every church on the island must have had bell-ringers on duty. Whistles blew; there was the popping of firecrackers, and possibly a gunshot or two. Sara heard it all in the background. The beloved features of Chris Latham loomed too close to consider unimportant matters.

"It's the new year," he said with an unreadable expression on his handsome face. "Happy new year, Sara." Slowly he bent closer until his lips touched hers.

Sara responded with no will of her own. At the touch of his lips she closed her eyes and his warmth spun through her body and sent her senses reeling. No thoughts, no pangs of conscience interrupted to stem the furious tide. She had no choice but to abandon herself completely to the will of the man she loved. Time had ceased to exist. The world could have ended while they kissed. Sara would never have known. Reality at last began to assert itself. Still held in Chris's warm embrace, Sara opened her eyes as their lips parted.

"My God, Sara!" said Chris, apparently as undone as she. Very slowly he released her, almost as though she had become a threat to him.

It was at this point that Mac discovered them.

Chris saw him first and quickly rose to his feet. With understandable guilt and incredible poise he said, "You do have an uncanny knack, old boy."

Sara could not guess Mac's feelings at this moment. He stood face-to-face with Chris, tense, but apparently not belligerent. Mac suggested evenly to Chris, "Hadn't you better be getting back inside? Michelle is expecting a kiss from her fiancé on this New Year's Eve." When Chris made no move, Mac continued, "And I am expecting a kiss from my fiancée." He looked at Sara, but did not smile. In fact Sara thought that he looked quite arrogant and cruel, an expression she had never noticed before.

"Sara?" Chris turned to help her up from the bench. Then he affably slapped Mac on the shoulder. "Come along, Mac. You are so right. We are being very impolite to the others."

"One moment," said Mac brusquely, ignoring Chris. "Happy new year, Sara darling," he said, drawing her into a crushing embrace.

Sara could feel Chris's eyes on them all during that long, fervent kiss. But it was as though Mac didn't exist. She endured the kiss and was grateful when he released her. Mac kept his arm around her waist as they returned to the ballroom. Chris followed close behind. Sara wondered if Chris could possibly feel as confused as she did at this moment.

Inside, everyone appeared to be kissing. "Happy new year" rang out again and again among the confetti and the confusion. Some guests even wore the silly hats that had been provided. Sara recalled other New Years when she had cheerfully worn the hats and thrown confetti. Now she felt only a numb despair as she made her way through the frenzied throng.

Sara kissed her father and Gwen. Michelle and Raoul had disappeared. Chris left, evidently in search of Michelle.

As the evening wore on Sara became acutely aware that Chris and Michelle had not returned. But she danced often with Mac and many others who cut in. Later they all went on to a small nightclub, dark and stuffy with cigarette smoke. A native band played music with a strong bass beat that gave Sara a headache, but she did not complain. Very early in the morning a flotilla loaded with passengers for their home islands left Tortola.

On New Year's Day no one at the Martine house stirred until after noon. While Michelle still slept, Mac and Sara had orange juice on the veranda. From idle chatter about the ball they had come around to the Lathams and Anne, Chris's late wife.

"How did she happen to be sailing alone? Was there a storm?"

Suddenly Mac lost his customary cool and snapped impatiently, "Sara, your morbid interest in the affairs of Chris Latham shall be satisfied. I am just the man to do it. In fact I shall tell you something that few people know about the noble Mister Latham."

Sara, taken aback by his hostile attitude, told him to forget it, but he would not.

"On the day Anne Latham died she was not sailing alone, as everyone thought. I was with her." To Sara's startled glance he replied, "No, not when she died."

Sara waited and said nothing.

"Anne was from a wealthy family, only child, headstrong, but very sweet too. Chris left her alone too much both here and in New Jersey. We saw them both places. Anne was never much of a mother—too much of a child herself."

"But she and Chris were very much in love," said Sara, knowing somehow that it was true.

"Yes, they were. And if it hadn't been for Chris's constant traveling, they would have had a good marriage. Anne was very lonely here. But she loved to sail." Mac paused uncertainly. "Sara, I told you once that I had never asked anyone to marry me. That was true. But I loved Anne Latham."

Sara's heart leaped. Mac and Chris. And now she had become a part of their competitive struggle.

"On the day that Anne died we had picnicked at a little secluded cove on Virgin Gorda. Much rum had been served—"

Sara recalled the day she had picnicked on a secluded island with Mac. Even then her intuition had told her that she was only one of many.

"Well, I made some passes," he confessed, "and she ran away from me. Anne took the sailboat, which was too much for one person to handle on that stormy day. I was miffed, and a little drunk, and I let her go. Then I stayed on Virgin Gorda overnight and didn't know until the next day that the sailboat had been found—empty."

Shocked, Sara asked, "Does Chris know?"

"No one knows for sure—except you and me. You see how I trust you."

"But, Mac, a woman died. Wasn't there an investigation?"

"The islands were even less inhabited then," said Mac. "No one had seen us leave. Anne spent a lot of time on her own, diving, sailing, almost always alone."

"She had a two-year-old child," Sara pointed out. "Why didn't she spend time with her?"

"Sara, you still don't understand." Mac brushed his brow impatiently. "Anne was not that kind of woman."

Poor Kathy, thought Sara. Now she was more convinced than ever that the child needed a good mother.

"The boat was found near the Dog Rocks," Mac continued. "Anne had been seen by a fishing boat out of Trunk Bay, a captain she knew. Anne waved to him, and that was the last anyone saw of her."

"And in all this time you never told Chris, or anyone?" asked Sara in amazement.

"Until today," said Mac complacently. "Which is probably why I drink, among other reasons." He went to the bar to refill his glass, omitting the orange juice. "Actually I'm not as bad as I sound," he said flippantly. "What good would it have done to besmirch the reputation of a dead lady?"

"She ran away from you," Sara pointed out.

"That day she did," said Mac. "But not on other days."

Sara stared at him in a kind of horrified awe, sadly disillusioned. "Why did you tell me?" she asked, wishing so very much that he hadn't.

Mac smiled—evilly, it seemed to Sara. "Chris hates me," he said smoothly. "Perhaps he knows, or only suspects, and now will never know for sure that there was something between Anne and me." Mac's fingers beat a tattoo on his drink. "What has Chris told you about me?" he demanded. "Nothing good, I'm sure."

Chris had been right. Mac was not the man she thought she knew. Sara replied truthfully in an almost strangled voice, "He said that you were his friend."

Mac had the grace to look philosophical.

Suddenly Sara had to get away from him. Michelle's sleepy arrival on the veranda gave her the opportunity. In her room Sara gave the Martines a lot of thought. She knew, unquestionably, that she could not stay with them any longer. Certainly she could hardly face Mac. Definitely she would never marry him. That was settled anyway. Sara had to talk to her father and Gwen as soon as possible. From her balcony she could see their houseboat still anchored in Privateers' Bay not far from the jetty. And Raoul Perez's large yacht still lay at anchor in the Marina Cay harbor.

Sara hurriedly changed into her bathing suit, threw some things into her beach bag, and announced to the Martines that she was going to the beach.

Mac sat brooding over his drink. If he had any thoughts about Sara's sudden actions or her reaction to his confession, he gave no indication. Michelle, still groggy from sleep or the lack of it, said nothing and waved her hand languidly.

Sara almost ran down the road to the beach. She felt elated, grateful for her escape. How close she had come to making a terrible mistake! Mac had taught her something. She wondered, with a chilling sense of loss, if she would ever get married.

Out in the bay her father's houseboat looked deserted, but then she saw movement on the forward deck. Racing to the end of the jetty she frantically waved her shirt. Captain Lamar waved back. Communicating by hand signals, Sara gave him the message that she would like to be picked up. Soon he was rowing toward her in the dinghy.

The captain had alerted her father, and both he and Gwen were waiting for her on the deck.

Her father said jovially, "Nice to see that my daughter hasn't forgotten our custom of calling on New Year's Day."

Sara had completely forgotten. Now she remembered that they always held an open house in Connecticut on New Year's Day. Suddenly Sara wished she were Kathy's age again. The grown-up world seemed too cruel, cold, and confusing. "Daddy!" she cried and burst into tears when he embraced her.

Gwen said diplomatically, "I'll leave you two alone. Some things to do below."

When Sara calmed down a bit, she told her father why she could not marry Mac Martine, now or ever. But still she told him nothing of Chris, nor Anne. Mac's secret would be safe with her. For he was right in a way: What good could come from repeating Mac's story of what had happened to Anne Latham seven years ago?

"Come back with us," her father was quick to say. "We'll stay for the Latham wedding on the third, but after that we'll be heading back to Saint Thomas, and home."

Sara said tremulously, "I don't want to spoil your honeymoon."

"Nonsense! This boat is too big for us anyway. Sleeps six, you know."

Sara hadn't wanted to stay for Chris's wedding—in fact, did not believe that she could survive it—but perhaps it would be necessary. Then she began to worry about Gwen, but Gwen soon dispelled her doubts with a warm, sincere invitation. And Gwen did not need a detailed explanation of why Sara was in such a rush to leave the Martine house, for which Sara felt very grateful to her stepmother.

Both her father and Gwen returned with her to the Martines', assistance that Sara deeply appreciated under the circumstances. Her father explained that they wanted to show Sara the American Virgin Islands on their return trip. Michelle seemed to understand the reason for Sara's sudden departure, but Mac looked at her quizzically.

Sara packed, carefully leaving the elegant silvery pink gown on its padded hanger in the closet, despite Michelle's urging her to keep it. Of course she returned Michelle's jewelry and placed both of the gifts from Mac in their boxes on the dresser. She wrote a check for the silver sandals and left it under a jar of cold cream near the jewelry. The amount, thirty dollars, was all she had in her checking account. She hoped it would be sufficient.

While her father packed her luggage and painting gear into the car and Michelle and Gwen stood outside on the patio, talking, Sara went to Mac, where he sat alone on the veranda.

"I was wrong about you," he said with no apparent

rancor. "I thought you wanted honesty, but you can't take it."

He was half right. Certainly she could not take him. "I'm sorry," she said. "Your jewelry is on the dresser in my room."

"Won't even let me make that gesture, eh?" he asked, gazing at her askance while he slowly tapped his foot on the floor. "If I go to hell, wrack, and ruin, you will be to blame," he said, sounding as though he joked. But Sara knew him now.

"You know who is at fault," she said calmly. "You know exactly what you're doing and where you're going. I can't wish you success in your mission, but I can't save you either. Good-bye, Mac."

"Cold lady," said Mac.

Sara did not look back, because he would see the tears streaming down her cheeks.

Stopping by the Latham house to leave the two portraits for Chris, Sara was delighted to find that Kathy's cold had improved. Mrs. Latham asked them to stay for tea. Sara had both dreaded and hoped to see Chris, but Nana said that he had a business appointment on St. Thomas.

"Kathy and I are in a dither today," said Nana. "After all, as you know, the wedding is the day after tomorrow, and I have the most terrible feeling that we won't be ready."

"You said yourself that Michelle is a very organized person," Sara reminded her. "I'm sure that everything will be just perfect." Even as she said the words they hurt.

"All those photographers," said Nana with a delicate shudder. "Sometimes I wish Chris had planned to marry a plain, ordinary girl, not a celebrity."

Kathy, who had been solemnly listening to the adults' conversation, said bluntly, "I wish he would marry anybody but Michelle."

All of the adults stared at the child in shocked silence. Sara was the first to recover. Reaching over to hug Kathy, she said, "Stepmothers may not be as bad as you think." Sara smiled at Gwen over Kathy's head and received an answering smile. "Sometimes they can be very nice."

"Not Michelle," declared Kathy fiercely. "She's going to be a really wicked stepmother."

At that they all laughed, and even Kathy smiled a little at her own fears.

Louella served the tea, and in reply to Sara's inquiry about the health of her husband, she replied, "He's keeping out of trouble."

Mrs. Latham again thanked Sara for her kindness in giving the portraits to Chris. "In my opinion you are an excellent artist, my dear. You make me look good, and at my age, that's magic."

"Thank you, Nana. But I'm still not entirely satisfied with your portrait."

"Then you must come to see me again," said Chris's mother.

Unlikely, thought Sara. She realized that she had been listening for the sound of Chris's Mini-Moke. But now the sun was setting and he still had not appeared. Sara's father said that they would have to get back to the houseboat before dark.

"Sara, swim with me tomorrow," begged Kathy, clinging to Nana's hip.

Sara waved to the little girl without committing herself. Tomorrow seemed only another impossible day to get through. All that she could think of doing now was getting away and forgetting.

CHAPTER TWELVE

Unaccustomed to the slow rocking of a boat as she slept, Sara did not sleep. Truthfully she could not blame the boat, but rather her errant thoughts. Morning light crept into her quarters, and she decided that she might as well rise and get on with the day—the second day of January. Tomorrow Chris would marry Michelle.

The sun, rising blatantly out of the sea behind the Jerusalems, reminded Sara that each day would continue to dawn—even without Chris—and she would have to get on with her life. She thought of Connecticut, where now the snow would be deep and the days gray. A sudden wild thought came to her that she should stay here in the islands and paint—paint it all—as she had once planned to do. But the spoilers had come: Mac and Michelle, and her own new maturity. Now the purity and simplicity she had at first felt here seemed to have left the islands. Now the conflict of reality and impossible dreams marred the pure colors of sand and sea.

Watching the sun rise higher, Sara picked up binoculars and trained them on Great Camanoe. Chris's Mini-Moke stood parked near the jetty, and the Bertram that Mac had borrowed was tied up there. No persons were visible. On Marina Cay a few persons sauntered along the beach. Many of the boats, which had been anchored in the harbor for the holidays, had now departed. Raoul's large yacht had gone. With binoculars Sara searched the surrounding waters, but his boat had definitely disappeared. She wondered when.

Her father appeared topside. "Morning, Sara," he said, kissing her. "You look about sixteen."

Sara, barefoot, in T-shirt and shorts, had not really bothered to dress. The faded old clothes matched her mood. She replied, "And feel forty."

"Now, now," he soothed. "What's so awful about a glorious day like this?"

Sara didn't wish to go into that. She suggested they have some coffee.

Her father picked up binoculars to follow a sailboat in Trellis Bay. He said, "One of those Capris out of Maya Cove."

"It's coming this way," said Sara. Training the binoculars on the sloop, she saw a large black man on the deck, then moving her gaze to the cockpit and the tiller, she exclaimed, "It can't be, but that man looks like Chris."

Chris Latham would not be handling the tiller of a sailboat. She kept her eyes on the man as the boat came closer. It was indeed Chris, with his dark curls flying in the breeze, wearing a blue-and-white-striped T-shirt that made him even look the part of a sailor. Sara couldn't imagine what had happened to get Chris into a sailboat.

In a daze Sara watched as the men prepared to anchor alongside. All three Willistons now stood at the houseboat's handrail. Sara felt so numb, and yet nervous, that she despaired of even saying hello.

When the two boats were within a couple feet of each other, Chris called, "Permission to come aboard?"

Grinning broadly, Sara's father replied, "Permission granted."

Chris bounded on deck. "Morning," he said with a wide grin of his own.

Sara thought how wonderful he looked: happy and rather mischievous.

"Sir, may I have your permission to take your daughter sailing today?"

Sara's father shot her a quizzical glance. "That's up to Sara."

"We're having a picnic lunch," said Chris. "Desmond, over there, will dive for the lobsters."

Kathy waved from the sailboat. "C'mon, Sara," she called.

"It's up to Sara," her father repeated.

"I'll get my bathing suit," said Sara.

In the cockpit of the sailboat named *Undine* Chris held the tiller. Sara sat, enchanted, gazing at his classic profile, feeling the strength and ease with which he controlled the boat as they flew over the waves. Amidships Kathy and Desmond were deep in conversation. Sara, content to be with Chris, did not ask about Michelle. The easterly trades filled the sails, and the water around them was the same brilliant blue as his eyes. Sara asked for nothing more.

"Lately I have been doing a lot of thinking about fear," said Chris. "And I realized you were right. I have been running away ever since my wife died. Running away to work, to travel, staying away longer, then feeling guilty because I left Kathy. You made me see it—the way I was limiting her life because of my fears and guilt." He stared hard at Sara. "Do you know that your eyes look violet-blue out here today?"

"Yours are the color of the sea."

He gave her a teasing smile. "Do you know that you have never said anything really nice to me before?"

Sara was startled. Hadn't she? Had she only been thinking all this time how wonderful, virile, and unobtainable he was? Had she really *never* said anything nice to him? A blush crept up from the low neckline of her T-shirt. Although Sara was certain Chris had noticed, he turned back to sailing, relaxed and competent.

"Sara, have I ever told you that you remind me of Kathy's mother?" Sara shook her head. "Your personality is different." Sara was pleased to hear that. "Anne was a beautiful, reckless girl. That was probably one of the reasons I married her. I was exactly the opposite. At first we were deliriously happy. Then with Kathy's arrival Anne wanted freedom more than ever, and I grew even more responsible and protective. Now I think Anne may have resented Kathy for spoiling our idyllic marriage."

Remember your marriage that way, thought Sara. *Keep your memory of Anne as a free, loyal, and loving wife. Never let Mac spoil it for you.* She said, "Anne must have been very lovely."

"Undine," said Chris. "That's the name of this boat. Do you know about Undine?" Sara shook her head. "Undine was a female water sprite who had no soul. The only way she could have a soul was to marry a mortal and bear him a son. Anne had a daughter."

"You have lived too long in the past," said Sara gently.

"Much too long. And except for you I might have continued. You made me aware that I was neglecting Kathy, depriving her of the freedom to grow in her own way, by saddling her with my fears." He smiled warmly. "Which is why we're sailing today. Now after seven years of fear and stubborn abstinence from the sport I love, here I am, and everything is right with the world."

"If I have done that for you, it makes me very happy," said Sara.

Desmond moved forward. They were approaching a cove with a white sand beach. Sara did not even bother to ask the name of the island. Because she was with Chris this island was Paradise and needed no other name. While Desmond searched for firewood, Chris, Kathy, and Sara swam and skin-dived, gathered shells and sipped lemonade.

Desmond captured two huge lobsters, which he tethered while he built the fire. Chris and Desmond broiled the lobsters while Kathy and Sara set out the rest of the picnic lunch: conch salad, fruit, and Louella's homemade bread. Tradewinds rustled the palms overhead.

"I want to say the blessing," Kathy said.

"A fine idea," said Chris, bowing his head.

Kathy repeated the small blessing and included a long list of persons, with the notable exception of Michelle.

After lunch Kathy wanted to hunt shells; Desmond agreed to go with her. The enormous black man and the little girl walked hand in hand along the beach, where the greenish-white water frothed lazily around their ankles, and they stopped often to gather in their booty.

Sara knew that she would never forget this last bittersweet day with Chris.

Resting under the palms, Chris said, "Do you remember how badly I behaved the first time Kathy said her little blessing?"

Sara confessed, "I was somewhat mystified."

"Kathy learned that simple little blessing almost as soon as she could talk. My wife taught it to her. She loved saying it at every meal, quite an accomplishment. But then, after her mother died, I couldn't stand hearing it. It brought back everything—the enormity of my loss. The blessing upset me so much that I asked her never to say it again. Kathy stopped saying the blessing that very day and she never said it again until your first dinner with us. I thought she had forgotten it long ago. That's why I was so shocked. Then, right there at the table in front of you—a stranger—everything came back to haunt me—all my mistakes in running away from Kathy, leaving her to be brought up by nursemaids. You must have thought me mad!"

"Thank you for explaining, Chris. Kathy is fine

now. All parents make mistakes with their kids, but they're not irreversible. And here you are sailing with her." Sara gave Chris a sunny smile. "Kathy is very lucky to have such a fine, understanding father."

Kathy raced up with a plastic bag full of shells. "Look! I found a pink ring." Chris examined the shell she offered. It did resemble a ring, mother-of-pearl on the outside, pale apricot inside. "Watch my shells, Daddy. I'm going to find some more." Kathy ran off down the beach.

Watching the happy, healthy child, Sara said, "What more could you ask?"

Chris grasped Sara's shoulders gently and turned her around to face him. "Only one more thing, Sara." His face was close and very serious. "I love you and I want you to marry me."

"Me?" Sara exclaimed, and the expression on her face must have been very funny, for he burst out laughing.

"Do you see anyone else around here?" he asked, his eyes flashing like sunlight on the sea.

"But you're marrying Michelle!"

"Not anymore. You haven't heard? Fantastic! And you came with me anyway, not knowing. Sara, my darling, forgive me!"

Sara merely stared in astonishment as he leaned over, kissed her tenderly, and sat back on his haunches to explain.

"We had a terrible quarrel about Raoul. Michelle said some pretty insulting things, comparing my finances to his, and then she admitted she never had wanted to be a stepmother. When she boasted that

Raoul had asked her to go with him on his yacht, I angrily told her to go. Then I realized I meant it. I wanted her to go."

Sara could hardly believe that Michelle would be so foolish—to give up Chris for Raoul. The woman must be mad! "I'm sorry," she said. "Maybe Michelle will return."

"Sorry!" said Chris, laughing. "You don't know how free I feel. I know now that I never loved Michelle. I want only you."

Chris drew Sara closer and kissed her, and it was New Year's Eve all over again. She returned his kiss with the full passion of her being, for now there was no thought of holding back. They loved each other truly and honestly for all the best reasons in the world and they would be married. They parted, only to touch again in loving wonder.

"I loved you the moment I saw you," said Chris, "your first day in the islands."

Sara, snuggled in the comforting curve of his arm as they leaned against the bole of the palm tree, said, softly teasing, "You fell in love with a half-drowned sea creature with stringy hair and sea-urchin punctures?"

"You made me feel protective," said Chris, lightly kissing her hair.

"And when you angrily told me that I knew nothing of tragedy, you loved me then too, I suppose?"

"More than ever, because I knew then that you cared about me—well, us."

"From the first for me too," Sara admitted. "But I

thought it was hopeless. What could I say? You had Michelle."

"And you had Mac. That was the hardest part for me to face. I kept telling myself that I was going to marry Michelle but that I had to save you from Mac somehow." He smiled at himself. "How we try to deceive ourselves! I was purely jealous. And Sara, let me tell you, there is no more excruciating pain in this world than for a man to see the woman he loves in the arms of another man."

"That won't ever happen again," Sara promised.

Chris again took Sara in his arms, and their kiss was a deep and tender seal of their mutual commitment. When they parted at last, Kathy stood beside them, a silent, concerned spectator.

"She must have said yes," Kathy commented.

Chris smiled at his perceptive daughter.

Without a word Kathy dropped to the sand beside Sara and snuggled against her. "Thank you, Sara. Now you can be my mother *and* my friend."

Sara kissed the little girl that she loved almost as much as Chris. "That's exactly what I shall be."

Chris reached over into Kathy's shells and extracted the pearly shell ring. He slowly slipped the ring on Sara's finger. "With this ring I thee wed," he vowed. "Now how soon can we make it legal? Wasn't there an emerald and diamond wedding band you especially liked?"

"No more than this," said Sara truthfully.

"We shall find the perfect ring for you," Chris promised.

"You found me," murmured Sara. "That's all that matters."

"I found you," Kathy corrected for the record.

Chris had the final word. "We found one another. And we Latham finders are keepers—forever."

Sara gazed up into the face of her beloved and was rewarded by the contented expression of a man who had at last come home.

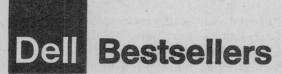

Dell Bestsellers

Love—the way you want it!

Candlelight Romances